HEIRS AND GRACES AT HIGHLAND HALL

HANNAH LYNN

Boldwood

First published in Great Britain in 2025 by Boldwood Books Ltd.

Copyright © Hannah Lynn, 2025

Cover Design by Alexandra Allden

Cover Images: Alexandra Allden and Shutterstock

A CIP catalogue record for this book is available from the British Library.

Paperback ISBN 978-1-83603-871-9

Large Print ISBN 978-1-83603-872-6

Hardback ISBN 978-1-83603-870-2

Trade Paperback ISBN 978-1-80656-045-5

Ebook ISBN 978-1-80656-045-5

Kindle ISBN 978-1-83603-874-0

Audio CD ISBN 978-1-83603-865-8

MP3 CD ISBN 978-1-83603-866-5

Digital audio download ISBN 978-1-83603-868-9

This book is printed on certified sustainable paper. Boldwood Books is dedicated to putting sustainability at the heart of our business. For more information please visit https://www.boldwoodbooks.com/about-us/sustainability/

Boldwood Books Ltd, 23 Bowerdean Street, London, SW6 3TN

www.boldwoodbooks.com

ALSO BY HANNAH LYNN

Hannah Lynn writing as H. M. Lynn

The Head Teacher

The Student

The Valentine's Date

1

Bex was sitting in the living room of the September Rose, with the log burner crackling away in the corner as Daisy recounted her latest escapades on the boat. Bex tried to laugh in the right places, tried to smile, to make it look like she was enjoying herself. And it wasn't as though she was having a bad time. She was spending time with her best friends – Daisy and Claire – whose company she loved, in a beautiful part of the country. But no matter how much she tried to be in the moment, it was hard when part of her mind was elsewhere. It always was now. Her head and her heart.

When she was at work, sitting in meetings where she would normally be the most vocal in the room, Bex now struggled to listen and instead stared off into space, normally spinning a pen between her fingers as she imagined him strolling around the Highlands. When she sat in her apartment in the evening, she imagined him going home at night to Kenna, his giant Maine Coon cat, or heading to the White Hart for a drink. Or maybe, just maybe, taking someone to The Haven, where they were about to experience their most perfect first date ever, the same way she had done.

It had been eleven weeks since Bex and Duncan had broken up. Well, almost. Technically, it had been seventy-four days. Seventy-four days since the longest, most uncomplicated and close to perfect relationship that she'd ever had had come to an end. She should have known, though, that it was too good to last.

'You're thinking about him again, aren't you?' Daisy's voice brought Bex back to the moment and when she lifted her head, she found Daisy glowering at her. Rather than responding immediately, Bex let out a long sigh. There was no point denying it, not to her best friends. They knew her better than that.

'I was just wondering what he's been up to,' she said. 'That's all.'

'Well, you could always ring him and ask,' Daisy replied, 'rather than sitting here looking like the most miserable person in the world.'

'I do not look like the most miserable person in the world,' Bex said with a pout.

'You're a pretty close contender,' Claire agreed.

With the distinct feeling that she was being picked on, Bex grabbed the bottle of wine and topped up her glass before taking a very sizable gulp. Like most weekends since the breakup, she was on one of Daisy and Theo's boats down in Wildflower Lock, meaning there was no need to worry about driving back to London.

'Look, I know you thought breaking up was the right thing to do,' Daisy said, 'but if he's half as miserable as you are, you've got to admit that maybe it was a mistake.'

'What was a mistake was thinking we could ever make something work long-distance, long term. I mean, it's not possible, is it? I spent more time on planes and trains the past year than I did seeing you guys.'

'And we were okay with that because we knew you were happy,' Daisy said. 'Sure, we missed you, but if Duncan is the one—'

'He is not the one. There's no such thing as *the one*,' Bex interrupted. She wasn't going to have them put ideas like that in her head, because the truth was, if there was a one for her, then surely it had to have been Duncan. In all her years of dating, she'd never had a relationship like it. So full of love and trust and complete commitment to one another. But then, if that had been the case, they would have been able to make it work, right?

They had known when they'd got together that it was going to be difficult, which was why they'd tried to keep things casual. Pretend they weren't falling head over heels for one another, but they had been. It was love, pure and simple. And that had been great while she'd been working in Scotland, but then, when she'd finished her work at Highland Hall, she'd had to come back to London. Somehow, they'd thought that love, and the willingness to travel, would be enough to make it work, and for a while it had been, but then the pressure began to take its toll.

Bex had taken a promotion at work – a promotion she'd got because of the work she'd done in Scotland – and while it hadn't been quite the leap up the corporate ladder she'd hoped for, and the damn corner office still eluded her, the job demanded an unfeasible amount of her time. Several train journeys and plane rides back up to LochDarroch to see Duncan had to be cancelled last minute, because of impromptu meetings, or brainstorming sessions that had run over, and when Duncan came down to London, she would often find herself tapping away at her laptop instead of heading out, or watching a film or simply enjoying the time together.

It didn't help that Duncan struggled with London life, either. He'd had fun the first few times he'd visited – she'd made sure of it. Shows, museums, trips on the London Eye. She'd pulled everything out of the bag and each time, he promised he'd enjoyed himself, but she knew what he meant.

He'd enjoyed visiting. Enjoyed spending time with her. But while London was somewhere that Duncan could cope with for a weekend every now and then, it wasn't a place he could ever imagine himself living. So the only option for them to have any hope of a long-term future was for her to move up to Scotland. To live in the tiny town of LochDarroch, but how could she do that when her job was here? Not to mention her friends.

It was just too complicated. Too difficult. That was what it came down to. And it was better that they'd ended things while they were still friends, while they still felt that affection – well, love – for each other, rather than let the obvious flaws in the relationship chip away until they became one of those bickering couples she always saw and wondered why they bothered staying together. No, it was better this way. The feeling of sadness would fade. The constant thinking about what he was up to and missing him so badly her body felt bruised would fade. Eventually. She was sure of it. It was just how long that was going to take that was the question.

'I need to ring Lorna anyway,' Bex said. 'I'll see how he's doing then. He might have moved on and forgotten about me already. I'm sure she'd let me know. Although she hasn't replied to my last message from a couple of days ago, which isn't like her. So maybe Duncan has moved on and she's too afraid to tell me.'

Lorna – Duncan's stepsister – had become one of Bex's firm friends during the four months she'd lived in Scotland the previous year. It had meant to be a two-month job, and when Bex had been assigned the position, she'd hoped to get it done even quicker than that. But then, when she and Duncan had got together, coming back to London hadn't seemed like such an issue. And it wasn't like there wasn't plenty to keep her busy. So she'd taken her time completing the task she'd been sent there for, sorting out decades of accounts for Fergus, the laird of the castle. She'd done a bloody good job, too. So good that the promotion had been waiting for her when she got home. And for a brief while, she'd thought she had it all. The career she'd been working all her adult life for, and the kind of partner she'd always dreamt about sharing her life with. She should have known it would be too good to last.

'You see, it's clear you're nowhere near over him,' Claire said, once again interrupting Bex's thoughts. 'I just don't want you to end up regretting this down the line. I mean, it's not like you considered all the different options, is it? Maybe you could have found somewhere else to work, you know. Got a transfer to another accountancy firm, maybe in a city.'

'There's no point going through this,' Bex said. 'I went through every option, and they didn't work. Breaking up was the only feasible thing to do. At least this way, we both have a chance of being happy.'

Claire opened her mouth as if she was about to say more, but Daisy shot her a look that silenced her on the spot. Thankfully, her friend knew when she'd pushed things too far.

'So, what are everyone's plans for the rest of the weekend?' Daisy said, her voice unnaturally perky as she topped up every-one's glasses. 'I take it you're staying here, Bex?'

'Just for the night. Then I need to head back and do some work.' Hopefully she'd be able to focus on it too. The fact that at least half her mind was constantly on Duncan meant she was far slower at getting things done than normal, and if she didn't sort herself out soon, she was sure her boss, Nigel, would notice.

'Amelia wants to drag me to that fair,' Claire said, replying to Daisy's question. 'I can't think of anything worse. Not in this weather. Do one of you want to go instead?'

Bex laughed. 'I think I might prefer work. Those fairground rides make me ill.'

'Whereabouts is it, and what time?' Daisy asked.

While Claire began telling Daisy the ins and outs of the fair, Bex was distracted by a sudden buzzing by her feet.

With a frown on her face, she pulled her phone out of her bag. 'I've no idea who would ring me at this time.' As she glanced at the screen, she got her answer. Her frown deepened.

'Everything all right?' Daisy asked, reading the confusion on her face.

'Sorry, guys,' Bex said, putting her wine glass down as she stood. 'I should probably go outside to take this. It's Nigel.'

'Nigel? Your boss? What's he doing ringing you at eight thirty on a Saturday night?'

'I don't know, but I guess it's important. I'll just be two secs, okay?'

'Sure. No worries, but use our room,' Daisy added, pointing down the boat to the cabin at the end. 'You don't want to go outside now. It's the middle of winter. It'll be freezing.'

'Thanks.' With a quick glance outside at the frost-covered grass, Bex walked through to the back of the boat, a knot twisting in her stomach. The girls were right. Her boss shouldn't be ringing her at this time of night. And given that she'd already got the promotion she wanted, it couldn't possibly be for something good.

'Nigel,' she said as she answered the call. 'Is everything okay?'

'Rebecca.' Her boss let her name out with a sigh that reverberated down the line. 'I'm ever so sorry to be ringing you so late, but I've got some news. Some terribly sad news.'

2

Bex was running late. She had booked the flight the moment she had got off the phone to Nigel, but she'd had too many glasses of wine to drive back to London, and even though Theo offered to take her, the last thing she wanted was him travelling unnecessarily back and forth on icy roads. Especially when she'd need to come back at some point to grab her car. So instead, she'd sorted the flight, then headed to bed with an alarm set for 6 a.m. Then she had driven back home as fast as she dared, considering the state of the roads, grabbed her things and gone straight to the airport.

Nigel hadn't had many details other than that Fergus, the laird that Bex had lived and worked for during her time up in Scotland, had passed away. He'd let her know as soon as he'd been informed, but he thought it had happened a couple of days ago.

A couple of days ago? The knowledge caused a tension to ripple through her body. Why had nobody contacted her? She had friends in the village. Good friends. At least that's what she'd thought. Although, maybe that was why Lorna hadn't responded to her message yet. Because she wasn't sure whether she was supposed to be the one to break the news or not. Either that or they'd assumed she was an out of sight, out of mind person. Which she absolutely wasn't.

'He's requested you go up there to work with the lawyer,' Nigel had told her on the phone.

'That's not normal, is it?' Bex replied.

'No, not really, but that's the information I've got. So he obviously wanted it. Are you okay to do that? You'll get paid, obviously, but that's not what I meant. I know you were very fond of the old man.'

'I really was,' Bex said.

Even after she and Duncan had got together, Bex had still spent a large amount of time at the castle, and not just working there. She had grown used to her large room with the four-poster bed, but even more so, she had got used to Ruby, the red Labrador, who had taken to her and slept on the armchair at the end of her bed at night. If she went more than a couple of days without sleeping at the castle, Ruby would get more than a little perturbed.

Unfortunately, Ruby wasn't the only one who wanted attention, and Duncan's Maine Coon cat, Kenna, insisted she got her fair share of love and fuss too. In the three months since Bex's last visit, there had been a definite furry shaped hole in her heart, as well as the one in the shape of the broad muscular Scotsman. A small part of her was grateful that she was going to get to see her animal companions again, although that meant she was definitely going to have to see Duncan, too. But for now, Bex was trying to push those thoughts from her mind and focus on getting to LochDarroch and learning why Fergus had wanted her there.

Normally, when she flew for work, Bex would always have the luxury of selecting business class, and it was a luxury she enjoyed, even on short flights. But when she had finally managed to book her seats at 10 p.m. the night before, economy was all that was available and for once, she didn't care. Getting to Highland Hall was what mattered. If they hadn't had a flight, she would have taken a train. She would have even contemplated driving again, which after her first trip up there, she'd promised herself she would never do again. But this was different. She just needed to be there.

With a small carry-on suitcase, Bex made her way through to departures and was standing in the queue when her phone started buzzing. She retrieved it from her pocket and felt a slight hitch in her chest at the sight of Lorna's name flashing on the screen.

'Bex, I am so sorry.' Lorna didn't even give Bex a chance to get a breath in before she started. 'I had no idea you didn't know. I thought Duncan would've told you. But then I should have rung and checked. I'm so sorry. It was only when we were talking this morning that I realised no one had spoken to you. I really had no idea you didn't know.'

'It's fine,' Bex said as Lorna's guilt bombarded her down the phone. 'I would have assumed Duncan would have let me know too, but hey, I guess things are different between us now.' A deep throb began behind her sternum as she realised just how different things between her and Duncan truly were. They would stay friends. That was what they'd promised one another when they called it a day on their relationship, and she'd wished with all her heart it would have been true, but deep down, even then, she'd probably known it hadn't been possible. How could you stay friends with someone who had been so much more than that for such a long time? After all, it wasn't like they'd been friends before.

Suddenly aware of the silence that had filled their conversation, Bex cleared her throat and carried on talking. 'It's all fine. I know now, and I'm coming up. My flight leaves in less than two hours.'

'Really?'

She nodded despite Lorna being unable to see. 'Yes. Apparently, Fergus requested that I work with his lawyer.'

'He did?' Lorna sounded as confused by this as Bex was. 'Well, when do you get there? I'll come and pick you up at the airport.'

'You don't have to.'

'I know I don't, but I'm on my way anyway. Mum wanted me to take her into town at some point this week, so she can go today. I'll pick you up, drop her off, then we can go back.'

'Thank you. That's very sweet. I appreciate it.'

It was only after Bex had hung up that she fully digested what Lorna had said. Lorna was going to have her mum in the car when she came to the airport to get her. Meaning Bex was going to have to face Duncan's stepmum.

As Duncan's mother had died when he was only little, Carrie, Lorna's mum, was as important a figure in his life as Lorna was. Bex had met them countless times over the previous year and a bit. Dinners out, birthday celebrations, summer barbeques, the lot. And they had always been incredibly warm and welcoming. Ideal in-laws, she'd thought at the time. But it would be different now, wouldn't it? Different now that she was Duncan's ex.

Trying to push the myriad thoughts from her mind, Bex readied herself to move through security. The queue had moved faster than she'd expected. Juggling her items, with her passport in hand, she barely looked at what was in front of her as she swung around, and as such, didn't notice that her suitcase was swinging straight into the path of another person, until it was too late.

'Oh God, I'm so sorry,' she said as the wheels collided with the man's ankles.

The man stumbled forward. 'What are you—'

He stopped mid-sentence as his eyes locked on hers. And what appeared to have been a scowl on his face faded as the slightest hint of a smile curled up on his lips.

'It's fine,' he said. 'No harm done. Although, you could've caused some serious damage if you'd wanted to. I never realised that wheely suitcases were such a deadly weapon before.' His voice reminded her of someone who would present the evening news. His British accent, crisp and clear, with every consonant enunciated perfectly.

'I'm so sorry,' she said, letting out a tight laugh that sounded unusually high-pitched. 'Really, I—'

'It's not a problem. There's really no need to worry yourself.'

She was staring at the man, she realised, and she didn't need to be. She'd said her apology, and he had accepted it, meaning it was time for her to move. But there was something about him that made it impossible to look away. He was about the same age as her, maybe a little older – mid-thirties, probably. His dark hair was thick, swept over to one side, and his jawline was so ridiculously sharp she was struck by the sudden urge to reach out and stroke it. Although she didn't think he'd be quite so quick to forgive that as he had been with the whole ankle swiping thing.

'Are you all right?' the man asked. 'You didn't hurt yourself, did you?'

'No, no, no.' A flash of embarrassment rushed to her cheeks. 'I mean, no, I'm fine. Yes, I'm sorry—' She wasn't sure whether she was making sense or not, but there seemed to be some sort of disconnect between her mouth and her brain. And the way his eyes twinkled really wasn't helping matters at all. Who on earth had eyes that actually twinkled?

'It's not a problem,' he said, again with that deep resonant tone. 'Not a problem at all. But it's your turn.'

'Sorry?'

'You need to put your luggage on the conveyor belt right here.' He gestured towards the security, where a wide-open space on the belt was awaiting the next piece of luggage to be scanned. 'May I?'

As Bex watched on, unable to swallow the lump that had filled her throat, the man stepped forward, picked up her suitcase and lifted it up onto the belt for her.

Bex didn't need anybody to carry her luggage. She was a strong businesswoman who frequently travelled for her job and never shied away from manual tasks, from moving desks at work to helping Daisy moor up her boats. Yet there was something surprisingly attractive about a man taking control in that way.

'I hope you have a safe flight,' he said, offering her another eye-twinkling smile.

'Yes, you too,' she croaked out, grateful that she'd been able to find her voice at least.

A moment later, the man was dealing with his own luggage, while Bex was left with an unusual feeling swirling in her abdomen. As she walked through the scanner, she cast a glance back towards the man, who was busy removing an expensive-looking watch from his wrist. It was just nerves at seeing Duncan, she told herself. Nerves at seeing Duncan, combined with the slightest hint of attention from an attractive man. An attractive man she was never going to see again.

At least, that was what she thought, and she actually managed to convince herself that was true until she reached her boarding gate and found him standing there in the line for first-class passengers. Of course they were on the same flight...

3

As Bex approached the queue of people, she considered veering in a wide path so that perhaps she could avoid him spotting her, but as he shifted his shoulders and the sparkling eyes landed on hers, she knew it was too late. And damn it if the butterflies weren't back again.

'This feels like you might be following me.' His lips lifted into a grin.

'I can assure you it's a coincidence,' Bex said, grateful that she had managed to speak properly this time. Although from the way the man's eyes narrowed, he didn't look convinced.

'Are you sure? I'm thinking that maybe you're some kind of secret spy who failed in an attempt to incapacitate me with your suitcase earlier, and now you've had to follow me onto my flight.'

As he quirked an eyebrow, Bex laughed. 'I like that. And to be fair, I think I'd make a good spy.'

'Is that right?'

'Well, apart from the different languages part,' she considered. 'I'd be rubbish at that. Maybe I'd be better as a computer hacker, one of those masterminds who moves money into

offshore accounts. Extreme tax evasion. Setting up shell compa-
nies. Those kinds of things. I could definitely do a bit of money
laundering, I think. I doubt it would take me that long to learn.'

'Wow. That's not something you'd confess to most strangers.'
He chuckled resonantly as Bex realised just what she'd said.

She shook her head. 'Sorry. Ignore me. I'm talking nonsense.'
Her cheeks flushed red. She was talking absolute nonsense, and
she had no idea why. She had spoken to plenty of attractive men
in her life and quite often they had been the ones who ended up
babbling in front of her. But there was something about this
man's sparkling eyes that was utterly mesmerising. And it didn't
help that an aroma of expensive citrus-based aftershave eddied
from his body. She could breathe in that scent forever. What the
heck was wrong with her? she chastised herself. Was she really
that desperate for a man's attention? Then again, before Duncan,
she had gone from one guy to another, always searching for Mr
Right, and each time they'd broken up, she'd bounced right back,
ready to continue the search. But this was different. This was the
first time she'd even found a man attractive after breaking up
with Duncan. And from the way he was continuing to keep the
conversation going, he thought the same about her.

'Well, I'm not sure if I'll ever need a money launderer, to be
honest,' he said. 'But then again, you never know. Those offshore
accounts sound good.'

'Until you get found out and slammed with an even heftier
bill,' she countered.

'Maybe you're right.' He grinned again. Yup, he was definitely
flirting with her. And what the hell? It was time she got back in
the game, anyway. A little flirting practice would probably help
her. 'So, are you travelling up to Scotland for something special?
To see a boyfriend, maybe?'

Any thought she had of flirting evaporated as her stomach

sank. 'No, actually, a friend has passed away. I'm going up there for him.'

'Oh God. I'm so sorry.' It was his turn to look embarrassed. 'I- I'm really sorry. I shouldn't have said that.'

'Don't be silly. Why would you have known that? It's fine, honestly. And I might actually bump into my ex-boyfriend while I'm there, too.'

'Ex?' His voice lingered on the word as he tilted his head to the side, that twinkle returning to his eyes ever so slightly. 'Well, if he's the one who ended it, he's a fool.'

He wasn't, Bex wanted to say. Duncan would have probably carried on as they were forever, not caring how resentful they'd grow of each other. Not seeing that it didn't matter how much they loved one another, it wasn't going to be enough to make it work. And God, she really did love him, more than she'd have ever thought it was possible to love someone.

As she looked back at the man, whose eyes were still looking straight at her, something heavy pressed down on her shoulders. Sure, it was nice that he was interested. Probably interested enough to give her his number if she wanted, but this wasn't the right time for that. Her heart was nowhere near ready for anything else. Even anything casual. In fact, casual had kind of lost its appeal now she'd had the real thing. And she may not have known exactly why Fergus had requested she went up there, but it was going to be work related. Something told her that dealing with the accounts of an estate the size of Highland Hall after a death wasn't going to be free of drama, and that was before she added Duncan into the mix. She couldn't deal with another complication right now.

'Well, I should leave you to board,' she said, flashing him a smile. 'It's a little while before they let the rest of us on at the back of the plane. Enjoy your flight.'

4

The flight was cramped, and Bex's mood wasn't helped when a man with a chronic cough took the seat behind her. As the crew were getting ready to take off, said man alternated between kneeing her in the back and coughing loudly as he lent forward so that his mouth was practically by her ear. In an attempt to block it out, she slipped in her AirPods and put on her eye mask and, as such, was surprised when what felt like only minutes after she'd closed her eyes, her body jerked upwards as the wheels hit the tarmac.

Not wanting to keep Lorna waiting, she was on her feet and pulling her suitcase down, ready to leave as quickly as possible.

As much as Bex knew that even taking a man's number would complicate her life more than she could deal with at the moment, she couldn't help but keep an eye out for the handsome stranger. But, as always, first class was long gone by the time she stepped outside. Part of her wondered if he'd linger a little, waiting for her to catch up. But then why would he when she'd made it very clear that she wasn't interested? This was better. Flirting could wait till she was back in London and her wounded heart had finally healed.

As the automatic doors opened and she stepped into Inverness Airport, a familiar face with piercing green eyes framed by long red hair waved at her.

'Oh my God, I missed you,' Lorna said, wrapping her arms around Bex and squeezing tightly. And for a moment, Bex let herself breathe in her friend. Lorna gave really good hugs. Not that her other friends didn't, but there was something about Lorna's that completely engulfed you, which was even more incredible when you considered how petite she was. Bex always thought it had something to do with her half-American side, though she'd never said as much.

'How are you doing?' Lorna asked when she finally let Bex go.

'Shocked. Definitely shocked. And you?'

'Same.' Lorna nodded. 'The village is in mourning, as you can imagine. I mean, it wasn't a surprise, but I think so many of us just thought he'd go on forever. You know what I mean?'

'I do,' Bex agreed.

She couldn't possibly have imagined that the last time she hugged Fergus goodbye, while he'd sat in his chair by the fireplace, would be the last time she'd ever see him. If she had known, she was sure there were things she would have said to him. Even if it was just thanking him for accepting her into his home.

'Where are you staying tonight?' Lorna asked as she made a motion towards the exit, with Bex stepping in line with her.

That was a good question. It seemed silly that she hadn't even thought about it until now.

'Well, my plan was just the castle. My old room, I guess.'

The way Lorna's eyebrow rose implied this probably wasn't as straightforward as she'd thought.

'I don't know if you'll be able to,' she said, an apology in her voice and expression, not that it had anything to do with her. 'The castle's locked up. They've been waiting for Kieron to arrive. I'm not sure when he's getting here.'

'Of course, I didn't think about that.'

Kieron was Fergus's nephew, and heir to the estate, but despite all the time Bex had spent at Highland Hall, she'd never met the man. It was safe to say that Duncan hadn't been his biggest fan, and from what he'd said, the feeling was mutual, and so any of his visits had conveniently coincided with Duncan coming down to London to visit her, rather than her heading up and meeting the source of his dislike.

'And to be honest, I'm not sure you'd want to stay in your room,' Lorna continued. 'The fires won't have been lit, and the weather's really turned these last couple of weeks. It's biting at the castle.'

'Right,' Bex said, her mind working through other possibilities. Obviously, Duncan's wasn't an option, but there were some B&Bs in the village, provided they weren't busy.

'Look, just stay with me,' Lorna said. 'I've got a pull-out sofa. It's comfy enough. When you remember to pull it out, that is.'

She offered Bex a slight grin as she said this, well aware that Bex had once fallen asleep on said sofa bed in an entirely inebriated state.

'Are you sure?' Bex asked. Lorna had already come all this way to pick her up. She didn't want to put her out even further.

'Yes, of course. The car's up here.'

Lorna wasn't joking when she said the weather had turned. Last time Bex had been in Scotland, a decent jumper and a pair of average socks had been more than enough. Now, after only a few minutes outside, her toes were already tingling and her teeth chattering. She would need to borrow some proper winter clothes, although it depended on how long she was going to have to stay, of course.

As they stepped into the car, Bex noticed it was conspicuously empty.

'I thought your mum was going to be with us,' she said. 'Did you say you were taking her to Glasgow?'

'Yeah, she wanted to stay there and do some shopping,' Lorna said as she opened the boot to put Bex's suitcase in. 'She'll get the train back. She doesn't like being on other people's schedules. Besides, I think she wanted to give us a bit of time to catch up.'

As a pointed silence filled the air, Bex was well aware of the one topic of conversation they were avoiding. There was a name that neither of them was saying. And as much as Bex didn't want to bring him up, she didn't want to feel the massive elephant in the room, either.

'So, how has he been?' she asked. Apparently saying Duncan's name was still tricky, but she didn't doubt that Lorna knew who she was talking about. And from the way her lips formed a thin line, it wasn't good news.

'He's struggling,' Lorna said softly. 'I've tried talking to him about it, but he's not himself. Not even close.'

A deep pain struck somewhere near Bex's sternum, and for once it wasn't only her pain. It hurt, knowing that he hurt. Knowing that someone she loved was suffering and she couldn't do anything to stop it. In the silence, her stomach churned.

She could still remember the stories about when Duncan's previous relationship – an engagement – ended. Lorna had told her all about how he'd turned reclusive. He wouldn't let anyone into his life. She prayed he hadn't gone back to that again, but it seemed to be his default. Shut out the world completely until you can cope with facing it again. And Bex understood. If it hadn't been for her job and her friends, she would have been tempted to do the same these last few weeks. She glanced at Lorna, forcing a small smile, only for her stomach to growl so loudly her friend's eyes widened.

'Hungry?'

'It was an early flight,' Bex admitted, placing her hands on her belly. 'Not much time for breakfast.'

'Then let's head to the White Hart. I'm sure they'll open the kitchen a bit early for a special guest like you.'

The White Hart was the first pub Bex had ever visited in the village over two and a half years ago. She'd gone there on a night out after being invited by Lorna and had fond memories of the evening. It was the first time she'd met Niall and Eilidh, Lorna's friends, and their attempt to make her feel welcome in the small village had been deeply appreciated.

But it had also been the night that Duncan had tried to use her to make his ex jealous. Now, they could laugh about it; it was amusing, the way he'd hopelessly flirted with her, not even sure whether it had just been to get back at Katty, or if he'd genuinely liked her. But back then, Bex had been furious that he'd tried to use her that way. It had almost erased the attraction she'd felt for him. Almost. He'd been too good-looking for that. Not to mention charming. And kind. And generous. But then, thinking about Duncan's good characteristics was the last thing she needed to be doing right now. She was here for work. That was it.

'Do you want to send Niall and Eilidh a message?' Lorna said as she drove. 'See if they want to meet us for food. As long as you want to, that is.'

'Absolutely. It'll be good to see them,' Bex said, before firing off a text in the friends' group chat, which they immediately replied to.

For the rest of the journey, they talked about bits and bobs; how the village was coping without Fergus, what was expected to happen to the castle. That sort of thing. Mainly, though, they kept the conversation away from both Duncan and Fergus. At least with Lorna, that was easy to do. She had so many adventures and plans on the go that she could easily talk your ear off about them.

The journey by car always took longer than expected. The ice on the road had made it even slower, and it was well past midday. So by the time they reached the village, Bex had learned all about Lorna's current plan: to move to America and open a traditional Scottish restaurant.

'Good, I'm famished,' Bex said as they stepped out of the car. Given that it was a Sunday and the White Hart was over half of LochDarroch's go-to pub, Bex only hoped that Niall and Eilidh had managed to grab a table before it got too busy.

Taking her time on the slippery ground, Bex began making her way to the door when Lorna's phone started ringing.

'Oh, it's Niall. They must be running late.'

She picked up the phone, but rather than speaking, she remained silent, obviously listening to whatever Niall was saying. As he spoke, Lorna bit down on her lip and glanced at Bex, her smile dropping as she did. Something in Bex's gut tightened. She somehow knew they were talking about her.

'Do you know what?' Lorna said as she hung up the phone. 'The guys were thinking that maybe we should go to The Haven instead to celebrate you being back. We haven't seen you in ages.'

'The Haven?' Bex raised her eyebrows.

The Haven was the most expensive restaurant on the outskirts of town and part of a hotel. Duncan had taken her there for their first date, and there hadn't been any prices on the menu, which in itself was an indication of how extortionate it was. The food had been incredible, but this wasn't a *Haven* kind of situation.

'What is it?' she asked, looking Lorna straight in the eye. 'Why don't you want to go into the White Hart?'

'I don't mind, it's just, you know. Cold. And musty. And the fires in there are so strong.'

'I thought you just said it was cold.'

'Right. Right.'

Lorna was a terrible liar. And although she was only Duncan's stepsister, they had a surprising number of traits in common, including blushing. With Duncan, it was the tops of his ears that went red. With Lorna, it was her whole face, which flushed bright pink.

'He's in there, isn't he?' Bex asked, suddenly piecing it together. 'Duncan is in there.'

'Look, we can go eat at the Boar, or we can make cheese toasties at mine. I'm sure I've got some food.'

A sad laugh escaped Bex's lips. She shook her head.

'Honestly, it's okay. Duncan and I said we were going to be friends. There was no bad blood in our breakup. It'll be nice to see him.'

Lorna's face remained crinkled with concern. 'I'm sure you think that now, but when you—'

'Don't be ridiculous,' Bex said, turning around.

Before Lorna could protest, Bex put her hand on the pub door. 'Now, are you coming, or am I going in on my own?'

She swung the door open, steeling herself with her best smile. She and Duncan would get on. They would be the perfect exes. She could feel it. Or at least, while she was here, she would play the part and then she would wait until she was back in London before she broke down in tears.

With her shoulders still pushed back, Bex stepped inside, just as a loud laugh rattled through the pub.

'Oh, you're just hysterical!' The voice had an Australian twang – probably one of the tourists who visited frequently.

Bex's attention was immediately drawn to the corner, where two women were sitting and laughing. Her jaw dropped.

The women weren't alone. Sat in the middle of them, with one arm around each of the young blondes, was Duncan. Drinks in front of him, their hands on his lap.

So much for thinking he'd become a recluse again.

5

Bex could feel her jaw hanging open as she looked at him. No, this Duncan definitely hadn't turned into a recluse at all. By the looks of things, he had been there since the pub opened that morning, although part of her couldn't help but wonder if he'd been with the Australian women before then too. One thing was clear, though. He was drunk, and she didn't need to see all the empty glasses on the table to know that. His cheeks had taken on a rosy hue, and there was something about the way he was grinning that felt overly forced – or at least alcohol-induced. As she stood there, he whispered something into one of the women's ears. The woman threw back her head and laughed.

'I'm sorry,' Lorna said. 'We can go. Let's leave now. We'll grab the others and get something else for lunch. Honestly, we don't have to stay here.'

Bex wanted to reply. She wanted to say that leaving was probably a good idea, as there was no way her fragile heart could cope with seeing Duncan like this. Seeing him so... so okay, after how she had spent the past few weeks. But her throat seized up, and her eyes were unable to look anywhere except straight ahead at

Duncan. Even as she felt Eilidh and Niall sidle up beside her, her attention remained locked entirely on Duncan. It was in that moment, as her lips parted, ready to speak, that he moved his head away from the pretty blonde at his side and looked at her.

The same level of shock that registered on her face appeared on his. Pure disbelief. Yet why would he be surprised? He was the person closest to Fergus, and as far as she was aware, nothing happened in Highland Hall that Duncan wasn't aware of. Had they not told him she was going to the castle? That she had been summoned? It certainly didn't look like that, though the expression of horror on his face didn't last long. As she stood there wondering what to say, his demeanour changed. And it wasn't a positive change. It was like a thundercloud had settled.

'Ladies,' he said as he pushed himself up from the table, grabbed his glass, then squeezed past the women, before swaggering over to her. There was a slight sway in his stride that might have been less noticeable if he wasn't such a tall guy. Or maybe it was just because Bex knew how he normally walked.

'What the hell are you doing here?' he said.

'Well,' Bex said, 'I'm sorry. I didn't realise I'd be cramping your style by turning up.'

His jaw feathered. 'That's not what I meant. You should've told me you were coming up.'

Tension rolled through Bex. The hurt that had pierced her heart only moments before transformed into something far sharper. 'Why?' she scoffed, staring up into those blue-green eyes of his. 'So you could stop your flirting and turn on the whole reclusive, heartbroken act?'

A guttural sound reverberated from the base of his throat. Was he seriously going to try to defend himself? Pretend that he hadn't had his arms all over those women? Oh, she would love to see him try.

'Look, we just came to get some food,' Lorna said, placing her hand on her brother's arm. 'We didn't know you'd be in here.'

He shook her away as he switched his glare to his sister.

'You knew? You knew she was coming and didn't tell me? You all knew?'

He cast an accusing gaze across their friends.

'I think this is something you guys should discuss without us,' Eilidh said as she and Niall retreated to their table, leaving Lorna to handle Duncan.

'I found out first thing,' Lorna said. 'A matter of hours ago.'

His glare didn't waver. 'You still could've told me. You should have told me.'

'Hang on a minute,' Bex said, interrupting. 'Don't have a go at her. If we're talking about telling people things, why the hell didn't *you* tell me what happened to Fergus? Three days, Duncan. He died three days ago. Did you not think I had a right to know?'

The mention of Fergus's name was all it took. In that instant, his demeanour changed, the anger washing away from him. In that moment, Bex saw how deeply it was all an act. How deeply the pain went. The girls were a distraction, but not from losing Bex. He had lost someone he had loved for far, far longer than he'd loved her, and it was a kind of love he would never be able to replace. A dull ache spread through her chest as she wished there was a way she could comfort him, but that was no longer her job.

'I thought one of the others would've called you and let you know,' he said quietly.

Bex blinked as a tear streaked its way down her face. Hastily, she wiped it away.

'You should've told me,' she said. 'You should've told me. But for what it's worth, I understand, and I'm sorry. I'm sorry for what you've lost.'

Duncan grunted before tipping his glass full of whisky into his mouth. 'I don't need your sympathy.'

Bex took a deep breath in through her nose, her nails digging into the palms of her hands as her compassion wavered. Being hurt didn't excuse being an arsehole, and she was doing the best she could to stay calm, but he was pushing all her buttons.

'Duncan,' she said slowly. 'I know you're going through a lot, but we said we were going to be friends. Remember? We were going to try to be friends.'

'Yeah, well, we said a lot of things,' he scoffed. 'And I didn't know you were going to turn up on my doorstep.'

'Look, I get that you're going through a lot, but that's no reason to act like a dick,' Lorna said, squaring up to her big brother, despite the massive difference in their heights. 'Now, we're getting food. You do what you like.'

Then, without another word, Lorna grabbed Bex by the arm and dragged her over to the table where Niall and Eilidh had been watching.

'Are you okay?' Eilidh said, immediately pushing a full glass of wine into Bex's hand. 'I'm so sorry. We did try to warn you.'

'It's okay. It's absolutely fine,' Bex replied, taking a large gulp of her drink and wishing her hand wasn't trembling quite so much, though whether it was from upset or anger, she didn't know.

As the conversation settled over the table, mainly centred on what her friends had been up to since she had seen them last, Bex couldn't help but keep looking at Duncan. She didn't want to. She wanted nothing more than to be fully present in the moment, with Lorna and the others, but as the waiter brought their food over, she couldn't help but notice how Duncan had moved over to the bar and was ordering himself the largest glass of whisky she had ever seen. Before he'd finished it, the Australians were on their feet and walking over, their hands all over him.

'So,' one of them said with a giggle. 'What do you think? Are you going to come back to the hotel and see our suite? We're sharing it. One double bed, but it's massive. Definitely room for an extra...'

Bex's heart clenched, tightening in her chest as if it refused to beat. She was going to pass out. Pass out or throw up. Those were the only options. With her food turning cold and her appetite gone, she sat there, lump in her throat, waiting to hear what Duncan said.

You don't need to hear this, she said to herself, about to look away, but that was the exact time he turned and looked at her. His gaze briefly caught hers and in that moment, three words filled her head. Three words she desperately wanted to shout at him, as if they would somehow make everything all right. But before she could even open her mouth, Duncan turned back to the women.

'Actually,' he said, his voice louder than necessary, as if he wanted Bex to overhear, 'I'm not in the mood today. Maybe another time.'

6

Bex was aware that staying at the pub all day wasn't a great idea. Emotions were high, and she was exhausted. But it wasn't like she had anywhere else to be. It was a Sunday and she wasn't meeting the lawyer until tomorrow morning. Not to mention, it gave her a chance to catch up with people. Not just the group, but others in the village that she had grown close to during her months living there. Like Roddy, who worked various roles, from barman to taxi driver, and Moira, who was widely assumed the oldest woman in the village and still drank like a fish while she sat in the corner, knitting. The fact her eyes were still up to creating such patterns was, in Bex's mind, no small feat; apparently her liver wasn't her only strong organ.

And so, she stayed, sipping her drink, trying to stay focused on what people were saying. Unlike the others, she couldn't blame her lack of concentration on an increasing blood alcohol level, though. She had switched to Diet Coke after the first glass of wine, partially because she needed to be clear-headed to meet the lawyer. Partially so she kept her wits about her when it came to a certain ruggedly attractive Scotsman.

It was a little after ten when Niall and Eilidh left together. One day, Bex was sure the pair would discover they were more than best friends, but when that was going to happen, she had no idea. She was about to ask Lorna if there'd been any progress on that matter yet, only to find her friend's attention was fixed on the other side of the room.

Duncan could barely stay standing. His entire body weight was propped up on the edge of the bar and the sway that had been subtle before threatened to see him fall on his face any second.

'I should get him home,' Lorna said with a sigh. 'You don't need to deal with this. Why don't I give you the keys to my cottage? You can go there and let yourself in.'

Bex looked at the size of Lorna versus the size of Duncan. He was probably double her weight and over a foot taller, too.

'There's no way you can manage him on your own,' Bex said.

'It wouldn't be the first time,' Lorna replied.

A deep ache spread through Bex's chest. Lorna really did adore her big brother, and she could hardly blame her. He was a great guy. When he wasn't a drunk idiot.

'It's fine. I'll give you a hand.'

Manoeuvring a drunken Duncan was hard, but harder still was trying to ignore the words spilling from his mouth.

'I should've known better,' he said as he sagged against Bex's shoulder. 'I should've known you'd break my heart. I should've known that I was more in love with you than you were with me. I should have known.'

Bex didn't want the remarks to get to her. She didn't want to feel them like needles in her heart, but she did.

'You were too smart for me,' he continued. 'I knew you'd realise it someday. Guess you've got yourself some highflying city boy again? Course you have.'

Bex gritted her jaw, fighting the words she wanted to spit at him. Fighting the urge to hit him hard on the shoulder just to stop his ludicrous ranting. She had loved him just as fiercely. She still did love him. But they had to face facts: their relationship could never work. Her whole career was down in London, and he refused to move. But it wasn't a conversation they could have while he was this drunk, nor was it something she wanted to say while Lorna was there.

'Can you grab the key from his back pocket?' Lorna said when they reached the lodge. 'I'm not sure I can reach it.'

Bex stretched her arm around and slipped her hand into Duncan's jeans. There was no denying that she'd always loved his backside. But she had never imagined the last time she'd have her hands near it would be like this. She pulled out the key and handed it to Lorna.

'Just brace yourself. For the chaos,' Lorna said.

Bex assumed she was talking about mess, and that Duncan had let his tidiness slip since they'd broken up, but when the door clicked open, they were hit by a barrage of wagging tails and slobbery tongues.

'What the? Ruby?' Bex said as she noticed her favourite red Labrador among the mix. 'What are you doing here? What are you all doing here?'

She dropped down onto her knees, and the dog buried herself in Bex's chest. Against all her better judgement, Bex felt the prick of tears behind her eyes. Her life with Duncan had been so different to what it was now and there was so much she missed.

'Kieron won't let them in the house,' Duncan slurred. They were the first coherent words he'd said that weren't about Bex and how she'd broken his heart. But they were just as bitter. 'I know he won't. He'd put them in the kennel. So I'm rescuing them before that happens.'

Bex looked at Lorna, who raised her eyebrow.

'Kieron's not a fan of dogs as pets,' Lorna agreed. 'He thinks they should all be working animals. But... I think Duncan might've wanted a wee bit of company, hence he took it upon himself.'

'I did it for the dogs,' Duncan muttered.

Bex had to admit she was impressed with the way Kenna stood among the new additions to the house. Then again, she was the biggest cat Bex had ever seen in her life, but that didn't stop Bex from scooping her up into her arms for a hug. If only a brief one. The last thing she needed was Duncan telling her she'd broken his cat's heart, too.

'Come on, you. Let's get you into the bedroom. Jeans off, top off, into bed,' Lorna said. 'I've got it from here if you want,' she added, looking at Bex as she steered him through the door.

'Thanks.'

It was one thing seeing her drunk yet annoyingly attractive ex-boyfriend – who, from the drunken words he was saying, was still as in love with her as she was him – but it was another thing to be stripping him naked and putting him into bed. She'd done that a couple of times in the relationship. As he'd had to do for her too, when she'd had one too many. And each time it had ended with laughter and kissing and promises of happily ever after. There would be none of that now.

So, she sat on the sofa and waited for Lorna to be done.

'Hey, girl,' Bex said as Ruby immediately came over and dropped her head on Bex's lap, causing the resurfacing of tears behind her eyes. 'Yeah, I've missed you too. A lot's changed, hasn't it? You're looking thin, you know. You missing Fergus?' While no reply came, other than a slow wag of the tail, it didn't stop Bex talking. It was what she needed. 'Don't worry. It'll be all right. I might not know how, but it'll be all right.'

For a few minutes, the pair remained there. Silent in one another's company, as if that was the best they could hope for. Bex suspected Ruby would love nothing more than jumping up on the sofa and falling asleep next to one another, and part of her wanted that too. But there was no way she could stay at Duncan's. Even on the sofa.

'He's already passed out,' Lorna said as she appeared from the room and yawned. 'Come on. What time is it? We should get some sleep too. You've got a meeting in the morning. I suspect it's going to be a pretty important one.'

7

'I knew it would be a mess, but I don't know... I just didn't expect him to be this bad,' Bex said as they walked home.

She'd been about to leave the lodge when she'd noticed a large box in the corner of the living room, with a wedge of fabric peeking out of the top. Intrigue had got the better of her, and as she'd moved a little closer, she realised it was full of clothes. Her clothes. Everything of hers that she'd left was shoved there in the corner of his room.

They had broken up in London, and after tears and hugs, Bex had told him it wouldn't be necessary to send her things down. After all, they were going to stay friends. That's what she'd said. And she'd believed that. She'd believed she'd be able to grab all her belongings when she next visited. But that visit had not happened.

She could hardly blame Duncan for packing her stuff up and closing the lid, the way he'd felt she'd done to the relationship, but seeing it there caused a whole new rawness to tear at her. They had been broken up for almost three months. How was it possible to be so unrecovered from a breakup after so long? She'd never experienced it before. But then again, she'd never been with someone for nearly a year and a half before.

On the plus side, at least it meant she had some warm clothes. Had it not been for the exertion of carrying half of Duncan's weight and borrowing Lorna's gloves on the way down, she probably would have frozen. So, after selecting a jumper, her biggest coat, gloves, scarf and hat, she had put the lid back down on the box and followed Lorna outside.

'I know, he's not in a great way. But you don't have to shoulder all the blame yourself,' Lorna replied.

Bex wasn't quite sure she agreed with that, but Lorna glanced across at her.

'He was away when Fergus passed,' she explained. 'He'd taken himself off somewhere, needed a bit of space. There was no phone reception. By the time he got back, he discovered he had twelve missed calls from Fergus, asking him to come back so they could talk. To say goodbye, I guess. Duncan never got that conversation. That closure.'

Bex covered her mouth as a searing pain throbbed in her chest and fresh tears trickled down her cheek. It was all very well Lorna saying she shouldn't shoulder the blame, but why had Duncan needed to take himself off for some space? She would bet her impressive promotion it was because of their breakup.

'I can't imagine what that must have been like,' she said truthfully.

Lorna nodded. 'I know everyone thought an awful lot of Fergus, but for Duncan, it was different. Fergus was as close as family. He was his best friend, grandfather figure, employer. And the fact Duncan never got to say goodbye… well, he feels guilty, you know. That he should have been there for the old man.'

That ache in Bex's chest was showing no signs of fading. Now it made sense why Duncan hadn't rung to tell her about Fergus's passing himself. It hadn't been about her, or how he felt. He'd had enough to deal with.

'God, poor guy,' she said softly.

'Right,' Lorna said with a sigh, before turning to Bex and offering a watery smile. 'But that doesn't excuse him for acting like a complete dick tonight. Those things he said, he knows they're not true. We all know how much you loved him. And why you ended things.'

It was a mutual decision to end things, Bex wanted to say, but she couldn't get the words out. There was too big a lump stuck in her throat, blocking them coming up.

'No. No, it doesn't.'

Bex's thoughts shifted back to her time in the castle. Back to Fergus. The three of them – her, Duncan and the laird – had developed a winter habit of drinking hot chocolate together in the drawing room of an evening. It was Fergus's favourite room in the house, and he had to have spent over half his time sat in the armchair next to the fire, the blanket over his lap. More than once, Bex wondered if, after she and Duncan had split up, it was a tradition the two men had continued. Part of her had even wondered if Duncan might consider moving out of the lodge and into her room just so neither of them was quite so on their own. But Duncan had never felt comfortable with the thought of living in the castle, even though she knew Fergus would have loved it.

With every step she took back towards the village, Bex considered how all these same thoughts would be eating away at Duncan. She just wished there was something she could do to help him, but she was there for a job, and he had made it perfectly clear that of all the people in the world, the one he would probably hate help from most was her.

8

Bex had arranged to meet Fergus's lawyer at the castle. Though she had never met the man before, she already had a strong vision of him in her mind. He would be Scottish, naturally, and old, probably not far from Fergus's age. It was likely that he'd known the old laird since childhood. That was the way it seemed with almost everyone there. Their lives were webs, the strands of which had been entwined since before the births and would continue that way for generations after their passing. It wouldn't have surprised her if she'd even met the old man more than once and not known what his role was, but still, she couldn't help but feel a bubble of nerves as she walked down the lane towards the castle, hoping that it was open and that she wasn't going to have to stand out in the cold and wait for too long. It was better, now that she'd got her gloves and coat, but that didn't stop the icy sting at the end of her nose or the way her breath fogged in the air in front of her.

Bex really wasn't sure how likely it was that the castle was unlocked. Lorna had said that Kieron, Fergus's nephew and the new laird, was expected to arrive from London any day, but there'd been no news yet, and the village grapevine would've normally been on top of such things, especially given the circumstances.

When she reached the castle, Bex stood out in the driveway. Ignoring the biting cold that stung the tops of her ears, she allowed her mind to be flooded with memories of when she had first arrived. She had assumed Fergus was the groundskeeper – with his tatty clothes, dishevelled hair, and the half-dozen dogs always around him. Then she had thought he was a grumpy old man with zero people skills. But it hadn't taken long before he had just become Fergus to her. Fergus, laird and lord to many, but to her, an old man whom she knew had suffered heartbreak, when he'd lost the love of his life in his youth. The ins and outs of that relationship – including whether it was the reason for his fallout with Duncan's grandfather – Bex couldn't be sure, but while Fergus had married, the conversations they had shared told her that his heart had always remained in the past.

As for other family, Duncan would regularly speak to Fergus's sister, though she didn't live nearby, and if what Duncan had said was true, the only times Kieron ever even came to Highland Hall was when he'd wanted to have some big party or host a fancy shoot for his London friends. She doubted he even knew the real Fergus – the man Fergus was to her. The one she'd share a hot chocolate with in the evenings. Who'd comforted her at the start of her and Duncan's relationship when her own heart had suffered a hefty blow. He hadn't even put up much of a fuss when his dog, Ruby, decided she liked Bex more than she liked him. He had only wanted what was best for other people. That was what it came down to.

With a heavy weight in her heart, she moved towards the castle, only to stop again.

There, just a little way off the drive, was a small herd of deer, basking in the pale rays of the morning light, a large stag standing in the middle of them all.

There was so much Bex loved about LochDarroch and the land around Highland Hall, but the wildlife had to be one of the main things. Deer, hares, foxes. She could have spent hours watching them. Although surprisingly, it was the birds she loved the most. From the dainty dotterel to the majestic birds of prey. She'd never seen a golden eagle before visiting here and even now she remembered the first time she had.

It had been her first summer, when she was still working on the accounts, and Duncan had surprised her with a picnic lunch. Given how wholeheartedly Fergus had approved of the burgeoning relationship, he'd given them the entire afternoon off, and the pair had headed down to the loch with a large blanket and after eating their food had lain down together and stared up at the sky. That was until Bex saw the giant bird and had leapt up from the ground.

'Is that... Is that... What is that? It's enormous.'

'That? That is a golden eagle,' Duncan had replied, wrapping his arm around her and pulling her back down next to him, so that her head rested on his chest.

'It's beautiful,' she'd whispered.

'Aye, it is. Special creatures, they are. Mate for life. Once they find the one, that's it. There's no one else for them.'

As she snuggled down into him, and watched the great beast turn in lazy circles in the sky, a strange feeling had settled over Bex. Like Duncan hadn't been talking about the birds at all.

The memory stirred a warmth somewhere in the pit of her being, only to evaporate as the image of Duncan, drunk with his arms around the two Australian women, resurfaced in her mind.

It was with a shuddering of her shoulders that Bex shook the feelings away and reminded herself to focus on the task at hand.

Then, with one last glance at the herd of deer, she headed over to the front door and, upon finding it unlocked, stepped inside the castle. It was eerily quiet. The grandfather clock stood where it always had, and the large oil paintings hung on the walls in time-less landscapes of the ever-changing views around them, but there was no patter of dogs' paws on the floors. No sign of life. Closing her eyes, she drew in the scent of leather and wood polish and a history she only knew a fraction of.

Quashing the melancholy that threatened to overwhelm her, Bex walked towards the study, the room in the house where she had spent months sorting through old paperwork, only to stop and change her mind. After all, she probably shouldn't just let herself into the house without knocking. It wasn't like it used to be. The new lord might not take kindly to finding a strange woman wandering around his home.

'Hello?' she called out. 'It's Bex. Rebecca. The accountant.'

'I'm just in here.'

The voice that answered took Bex by surprise. First, it was coming from the drawing room, the small room next to the main staircase – where Fergus would sit in the evenings with a dram of whisky and his dogs. It was the homeliest room in the castle, and certainly not where she expected to be doing business with the lawyer. The study would have been a much better fit, and assuming the lawyer was an old friend, she'd thought he would know that. But the second thing that surprised her was that the lawyer sounded English. Not a hint of a Scottish accent anywhere. He also sounded younger than she had expected.

Another person sent up from London to get the job done? Possibly. And there was no point delaying it any further.

With a sense of sadness she knew would come with seeing Fergus's room, she pushed open the door to the drawing room, only to be hit with a spark of anger.

The lawyer, whoever he was, had his back to her. He had picked up a chair and moved it so that it was directly in front of the fire. Only it wasn't just any chair he'd taken and turned. It was Fergus's armchair. The one he'd always sat in. And to make matters worse, the old tartan blanket that Fergus had kept across his lap had been tossed aside onto another chair with half of it dangling on the floor, like it was meaningless.

'Sorry, but you shouldn't be sitting there,' Bex said.

'Excuse me?' the voice said, nothing but his expensive shoes visible.

'I said you shouldn't be sitting there. That's Fergus's chair and you should have left it where it was. It's a matter of respect.'

As the man rose leisurely to his feet, Bex's frustration rose. 'Did you hear what I said? I said you need to put that chair back where it belongs.'

She stopped as the man turned slowly to face her, almost as though he was toying with her. The heat of anger bubbled to burning, but as his eyes met hers, words stuck in her throat.

'It's you,' she choked out, struggling to make sense of who she was seeing. 'You're the man from the airport.'

His eyes twinkled in the exact same way they had done the day before. 'And you're the woman who nearly gave me a broken ankle.'

9

He was just as good-looking as Bex remembered. Possibly more so. Dressed in a light-blue checked shirt with the top button undone, he looked as though he'd just finished work in the office and removed his tie. Except, of course, that couldn't be the case, given it was first thing in the morning.

A lawyer and an accountant. That was a better match. A match that made more sense than an accountant and a groundskeeper, didn't it?

As quickly as the thought shot into her head, she tried to shove it away. No, she wasn't going to be having thoughts like that. She was here to work with him, that was all. Besides, if the night before had taught her anything, it was that she was 100 per cent not over Duncan. Not taking this man's number had been the sensible thing to do, but of course, that had been before she was going to know she had to see him again. Work with him even.

As she stood there, her jaw still slightly open, she couldn't help but wonder if fate was playing some dark, twisted joke on her.

'So, you're Rebecca,' he said, a small smile tugging at his lips accentuating the glimmer in his eye. 'The phenomenal accountant I've heard so much about.'

'Well, I wouldn't say phenomenal,' Bex said, before inwardly wincing at how bashful she sounded. That wasn't a normal start at all. No, she was proud of how capable she was. She cleared her throat and started. 'But yes, I'm the one who sorted out all the finances at the estate for Fergus before he passed away.'

The man nodded. 'From what I hear, the old man was very fond of you. I'm getting the feeling it was mutual, what with you trying to kick me out of his chair and everything.'

'Yes, the chair.' Just because he was good-looking didn't mean she wasn't still annoyed. 'That was his favourite place to sit in the evenings,' she said. 'We used to sit there together. Have a drink. A hot chocolate normally.'

'With a dash of something in it, I'm guessing,' he said, his smile tilting slightly to the side.

A whole swarm of butterflies took hold of Bex's stomach. My God, he was charming. And he knew it. She could tell. You didn't look like that without knowing about it. And obviously, he was intelligent. He wouldn't be working on a case like this if he weren't.

But she wasn't going to get sucked in by that. She'd been sucked in by enough men like him in the past. She wasn't going to make that mistake again. That's why being with Duncan had been so refreshing; because he hadn't bought into that fast car, lavish luxury lifestyle. He knew it was the little things that mattered more.

'Well, I guess we need to get started on work,' she said. 'I'll be honest. I have no idea why Fergus wanted me here. I thought I'd done my job and this type of thing would fall on you.'

'We?' The man's eyes narrowed.

'Well, I didn't know it would be you exactly,' Bex said, wishing his eyes would stop that damn glittering thing they were doing. 'I actually imagined he'd have employed some old local lawyer to do the job instead.'

The man's lips parted into a slight O shape. 'Oh, you think I—'

Whatever it was he was going to tell her, he was cut off when her phone rang loudly in her bag.

'Sorry,' Bex said, offering an apologetic smile before pulling out her phone and staring at the screen. It wasn't a number she recognised.

'Hello?' she answered.

'Hello, Rebecca? It's Gordon here.'

The voice on the other end of the line carried a thick Scottish accent.

'Gordon?' she said.

'The lawyer. I was meant to be meeting you at the castle today. I'm awful sorry, I'm running late. Bloody sheep on the road. I'll be about another forty minutes.'

'You're the lawyer,' she repeated. A prickling sensation rose on the back of her neck.

'Aye, are you already there? The nephew arrived last night. Should be able to let you in if you are.'

'Right...' Her throat was so dry she couldn't even answer his question about whether she was at the castle yet, let alone say goodbye before he hung up.

She turned back towards the room, her eyes settling on the man who, only minutes ago, she had assumed was the lawyer she was meeting.

'You're not the lawyer,' she said, still trying to swallow a lump that was trying to stick in her throat.

'No,' he replied, the slightest hint of a smirk on his lips.

'Which means you're...'

'I'm Kieron,' he said, the smile widening. 'The new laird.'

Bex felt like an idiot. A complete and utter fool. How had she mistaken the new lord – and owner of the land and the castle – for a lawyer? Of course he wasn't a lawyer. He was gorgeous and charming and not even Scottish. At least, not Scottish sounding. Was this worse than when she'd mistaken Fergus for a groundsman? Probably not, but she'd never actually said to Fergus that was who she'd assumed he was.

'I'm so sorry,' she said, her words tumbling out. 'I'm ever so sorry. I seem to have got confused.'

'It's no problem. I was going to point it out, but then you took the call and it appears they cleared it up for you. I'm assuming that was the actual lawyer.'

'Yes. Yes, it was.' Bex nodded. Her stomach clenched so tight she wanted the ground to swallow her up.

'Besides,' Kieron continued, 'it was lovely to see how warmly you spoke of my uncle. I understand why he was so fond of you.'

He kept looking at her with that same warm smile, and though she wouldn't have previously thought it possible, that twinkle in his eye was even greater than it had been before.

'So, did that actual lawyer say anything of interest?' he asked. 'Anything I should know?'

'No,' Bex said. The lump in her throat had finally dispersed, although she wasn't sure whether her overheated state was coming from the fact that she was still wearing a coat, inside a room with a roaring fire going, or because of the way those eyes were continuing to look at her. 'He was just saying he'd be late. About another forty minutes or so.'

'Hmm, that is late,' Kieron pondered, pressing his lips together. 'I guess I should have known that was how it would be around here. Well, as we've got time to spare, I quite fancy breakfast. If you haven't eaten already, I'd be more than happy for you to join me?'

'No, no, I haven't,' Bex said, horrified by just how quickly her words came out. Though Kieron merely smiled at her response.

'Good. I was hoping you'd say that.' His smile stretched into a grin. 'How does smoked salmon and scrambled egg sound?'

'Smoked salmon and scrambled egg sound perfect,' she said.

10

'I'm not sure if you'll find much down here,' Bex said as they walked down to the kitchen. Fergus had never been one for keeping food in the house. In fact, he'd insisted on eating out at a different restaurant, pub, or café every day, claiming it was his way of supporting the community. The fact that he was the landlord to most of those establishments didn't seem ironic to him in any way.

'So, you already know about my uncle's habit of not having food in the house,' Kieron said. 'Don't worry, I came prepared.'

'I managed to break it a little bit,' Bex said. 'I persuaded him to at least keep bread in for toast, just so that he didn't exist solely on whisky in the evenings when he didn't go to the pub. And he would join me and Duncan for dinner when Duncan cooked here too.'

'Duncan cooked in the castle? The groundsman?'

'Well, he and Fergus were very close,' Bex said, hoping she could skim the conversation around that particular person, but she could already feel that Kieron had latched on to him.

'Yes, I heard as much,' he said, his tone laced with the

slightest of edges. 'And what about you and Duncan? Were you two... friends?'

There was something about the way he said the word 'friends' that made it apparent exactly what he was saying. Then again, she was the one who'd told him she might bump into her ex while she was here.

'We were,' she said, wondering if he could read between the lines.

His lips pressed tightly together before the tension released, and they curled up into a smile. 'Well, let me get started on some food.'

As he cracked eggs into a pan, he moved the conversation to a standard level of small talk.

'So, were you and your uncle close?' Bex asked. 'I mean, I never saw you when I was here.'

'No, and what a shame that is. Unfortunately, my visits were always fleeting. You know what it's like when you have a busy job. You can't just spend your days strolling around the countryside, no matter how much you might like to.'

Was that a dig? she wondered. At Duncan or even Fergus, perhaps? Or was she just reading too much into it? That seemed a more likely explanation.

'What is it you do?' she asked as she leaned against the countertop. 'Now that I know you're not a lawyer.'

'No, no.' He flashed her a grin as he continued to stir the eggs. 'I work in banking.'

She raised an eyebrow. There were so many men in London who had used 'banking' as a vague umbrella term for whatever it was they did. Some seemed to classify everything from working as a teller to being a top hedge fund manager under the same label. Somehow, though, she didn't think Kieron was the type to be working behind a counter in a bank.

'I'm sorry you had such a mess to deal with when it came to the old man's accounts,' he said. 'I'd been on at Fergus for years to sort it out. I even bought him a computer. Though my mother suspected he just used it as an oversized paperweight.'

'I don't feel like I should comment here,' Bex said with a small laugh.

'Do you know where the plates are? Could you get me some?' he asked.

'Sure thing.' Bex moved over, instinctively getting plates and cutlery from the drawers the way she had done before.

'And the salmon's in the fridge,' he told her. 'If you could grab that, too.'

A few minutes later he sprinkled some finely chopped spring onions onto the scrambled egg; it looked like the kind of meal she'd have paid a fortune for at a café in London.

'I'm afraid it's nothing special,' he said.

'Thank you,' she said, taking her plate and moving over to the small table. It was a long way from the dining table upstairs that had to be able to seat at least twenty people, but she'd had a lot of laughs around it. 'This is absolutely delicious,' she added, trying to focus on current company and not relive the past.

'So, I guess if you're the person Fergus insisted on having here, you must be a director at your firm,' Kieron asked as he took a bite of his food.

'No,' Bex replied. 'I'm a senior manager.'

'Manager, not director? With a big job like this?'

She shrugged, hoping she didn't show quite how much the comment irked her. It wasn't Kieron's fault, after all. She had hoped to be at the director level by now, with a nice corner office and views out of London, and she had been given a promotion up to senior manager when she'd finished the job before, but it sometimes felt like the directors at the firm were an old boys' club, and being neither old nor a boy, she wondered if the powers that be would ever even notice how much she deserved the role. 'Director is not an easy position to get in my job,' she said diplomatically. 'A lot of it is about longevity. You know, how many clients you bring in and how long they stay.'

'I've got a lot of friends in London who could use your help. If you don't mind me passing them your name? In fact, I think I probably owe you that. I'm sure that what I'm inheriting would be a hell of a lot harder to deal with if you hadn't done all that work for him last year.'

The sheer scale of what Kieron was inheriting was almost too much to comprehend. Yes, there was the castle, but there was also the land, the establishments and the businesses Fergus had owned, which stretched far beyond the village. Fergus had employed only a few people in the house, but that was possibly because he had employed half the village elsewhere. All of their futures would now be in Kieron's hands. It was a struggle to understand how he'd ever get to grips with it. Especially considering he wasn't even from the area. The weight of that pressure must be mammoth, though if he felt that, he was doing a good job of hiding it.

'I have a few friends in similar situations,' Kieron continued. 'Old parents or grandparents – landowners who've let their finances get away from them. It'd be helpful for them to know someone with experience on a scale like this. Especially someone as respected as my uncle.'

'Then yes, absolutely,' Bex said. 'I'd be really grateful if you passed on the firm's details.'

She had just about finished the last bites of her breakfast when the sound of footsteps upstairs caught her attention.

'Gordon got here quicker than I thought he would,' she said, glancing at her watch. It had only been thirty minutes since he had rung. But that was the thing about travelling in the High-lands – you never knew if a journey would take twenty minutes or two hours. Sheep, roadblocks, village parades could send every-thing into turmoil. 'I should go upstairs and meet him,' she said, standing up and taking her plate, but before she'd even taken a single step from the table, the kitchen door swung open.

And it wasn't Gordon who walked in. It was Duncan.

11

The effects of the previous night's drinking were clear. Duncan was a bleary-eyed mess, with bags under his eyes and a stagger to his walk. Not to mention his fingers were pressed into his temples, the way he always did when he was struggling. He was so distracted he didn't even notice Kieron and Bex there until Kieron cleared his throat.

'Good morning?' Kieron said, his eyebrows raised. Duncan's head snapped around towards them, but rather than responding to Kieron, or even acknowledging that he was there, his gaze went straight to Bex. His whole body jolted, as if her presence had given him an electric shock.

'What are you doing here?' he said.

Bex felt her throat tighten.

'Kieron was just making me breakfast,' she said. 'The lawyer was late, and so we had time...' She trailed off, unsure why she was explaining herself to him. She didn't need to explain anything. Yet she didn't want him to think she and Kieron had been sitting there, simply enjoying each other's company. Even though that was what they had been doing.

'Duncan,' Kieron said, standing up and walking over to shake his hand. 'I wondered when I'd see you. I hear you're the one who put the dogs in the kennels for me. I appreciate that. I don't know why my uncle used to keep them in the house. Horrible habit.'

'Right,' Duncan said, his eyes flicking to Bex.

She didn't know how much of last night he remembered, but it was clear he was aware she knew the dogs had not been in the kennels.

'Well, I've just come to get them some food,' he said. 'It's still up here.'

'Right, well, don't let us interrupt you,' Kieron said.

Duncan moved slowly towards the fridge, pulling out the packets of raw meat Fergus had insisted on feeding the animals.

A strange, static tension filled the room, and Bex couldn't help but wonder if Kieron could feel it too. Her plate was still in her hands, and part of her wanted to move over to the sink so that she could wash it up, but that would mean moving closer to Duncan, or at least drawing his attention back to her, and that wasn't something she wanted to do. Not here. Not like this. And so she remained standing there, silent, waiting for the moment to pass.

'You might as well take enough for a while,' Kieron said as Duncan went to close the fridge. 'You know, so you don't have to bother yourself coming up here.'

Duncan grunted in reply as he opened the fridge back up. As much as Bex wanted to believe it was the hangover alone that was causing him to react in this way, she suspected it wasn't the case.

Finally, after what felt like an age, Duncan's arms were laden full of food. For the second time, he closed the fridge, then turned back to face them.

'Well, I should leave you two to it,' he said. 'Sorry if I interrupted anything,' he added as his eyes locked on Bex's. Her throat was bone dry, but she refused to break his glare. Her entire body was torn. Half of her wanted to run over and wrap her arms around him, and the other half wanted to scream at him for being such an impossible idiot. Couldn't he see that she was hurting just as much as he was? The silence had reached an unbearable level of tension, and she was certain Kieron was about to say something when Duncan finally swivelled on his heels and left.

As the kitchen door slammed shut, the tension roiled from her body, and it took all her restraint not to let out a sigh of relief. How did he do that to her? How was it so hard to be near him and not be with him? Whatever job this was the lawyer had for her, one thing was clear. She needed to get it done and get out of here as soon as possible. And as for the possibility of her and Duncan ever being friends? Well, it was safe to say that was definitely not going to happen.

'Honestly,' Kieron said, taking Bex's plate from her as he gave a roll of his eyes. 'I will never understand why all the village women are crazy about that man. He's practically a neanderthal. I mean, he can't even string a sentence together.'

'Right, of course,' Bex said, not even hearing what he was saying as her eyes remained on the door Duncan had just walked through, wishing she didn't want to run straight after him quite so much.

12

'Why haven't you kept the dogs in the house?' Bex asked as they made their way back to the drawing room. Kieron had washed up the plates while she dried them and put them away. Part of her wondered if he'd asked her to do that because he wasn't sure where everything belonged. Then again, why would he? He hadn't lived in the house yet. Would he know? In her mind, inheriting a place like this and not living in it would be absurd, but if he was a man who liked city life, the adjustment would be tough. She knew that better than anyone. 'I'm guessing you're not a dog person.'

'Oh, I love dogs, absolutely. But they're not house pets,' Kieron said as he opened the door for her to step through. 'Especially not dogs like those. They're so much better off outside in the kennels. Not to mention the house stays much cleaner that way. And you don't have to worry about ticks and fleas and all that nonsense. I mean, they have a good life. They're well fed. Get good walks. And they love it when I take them on shoots.'

'Clay pigeon shooting?' Bex asked. Duncan had taken her clay pigeon shooting several times during her relationship, though her most memorable time had definitely been the first one. They hadn't been together then – they hadn't even been on their first date – and even now she remembered the way her pulse had soared when he'd wrapped his arms around her as he taught her how to hold a gun.

'Only if I must,' Kieron said in response to her question. 'I prefer the real thing. Grouse, partridge. Sometimes the odd pheasant shoot when I'm down south as well.'

'Oh. Real animals,' Bex said.

She didn't know why this comment disappointed her. After all, almost all the gentry did that sort of thing, didn't they? And it wasn't like she was a vegetarian. She ate meat. Wasn't it better to eat animals you shot yourself? She tried to play devil's advocate, but it was tough. It was just something she could never imagine herself doing, that was all.

'So, is your plan to move into the castle?' she asked, steering the conversation in a different direction.

'Ideally,' Kieron said, the rounded tone of his vowels incredibly alluring. 'I mean, it's a dream, isn't it? Everyone's dream. The perfect place to raise a family. Assuming I find myself the right woman, that is.' He looked at her with a twinkle in his eyes.

Was he flirting with her? Yes, of course he was. The attraction had been there in the airport too, and it hadn't just disappeared now she knew who he was. But as Bex felt a flutter in her stomach, she was immediately annoyed at herself for it. She was here to work. She was a professional. Not to mention, Kieron deserved more than to be her rebound and at the moment, that was all she could offer any man. Still, it was hard to stop the colour rising to her cheeks and the undeniable fruition of tension building between them. Tension she had no idea how she was going to break. She swallowed, desperately trying to think of something to say, when the click of the front door rang out in the hallway.

'Hello, sorry I'm late. I'm here, I'm here!'

The deep Scottish accent that Bex now recognised as Gordon's voice bellowed through the house.

'We're just in here,' Bex called as they moved into the hallway.

Gordon was everything she had imagined: old, with grey hair and frameless glasses perched on the end of his nose. He was dressed in a thick tweed suit and holding a large briefcase in his hand.

'I'm ever so sorry. I should've left earlier. Rebecca,' he said, holding out his hand to shake hers.

'Bex,' she said. 'Please call me Bex.'

'Aye, right you are then, Bex.'

She liked him. It sounded ridiculous, but there were so many men she met on jobs who looked at her with confusion when they realised there was a woman on the project. The fact that she knew more about what she was doing than 90 if not 100 per cent of the men she worked with didn't seem relevant to them. Gordon didn't give that impression at all.

'Grand to meet you in person,' he said. 'Fergus spoke ever so warmly of you. E'er so warming. I'm so sorry for your loss.'

'And for yours,' Bex said.

Gordon turned his attention to Kieron, who was standing straight backed beside her. 'Oh, and you must be Kieron.'

'Yes,' Kieron said, flashing a quick smile. 'The new laird.'

Bex couldn't be sure, but she felt as though Gordon's posture stiffened slightly and the smile that had previously been flustered, yet relaxed, tightened.

'Well, I guess it's time Bex and I got on with some work,' Gordon said.

'Well, I thought I'd stay, if that's all right,' Kieron said. 'It *is* my future you're going to be discussing. In *my* castle.'

There was no denying it this time; Gordon's smile strained. And Kieron noticed it too.

'I'm the only heir,' Kieron said, enunciating his words clearly as he flashed what was clearly one of his most charming smiles. 'There's no one else, unless you're telling me he left it all to some charity,' he added with a chuckle. 'And I don't think Fergus would do that.'

Gordon let out a deep, laboured laugh. 'No, nothing like charities. But you know how these things work. All cloak and dagger until everything is officially sorted. Don't worry. I'm sure everything is in order. I'm afraid it'll just be the two of us at this point.'

'I see.' Kieron sniffed. 'Well, I trust that you know what you're doing.'

With another tight smile, Gordon turned back to Bex. 'Right,' he said. 'Shall we go into the study?'

Bex glanced at Kieron, feeling guilty that he was being excluded from the conversation. After all, it *was* his inheritance they were discussing. But Gordon clearly knew what he was doing, and she didn't want to complicate the matter further.

'I'm sure I'll see you later,' she said, unsure why she felt the need to say such a thing.

'I guess we'll see,' Kieron replied, then turned and took a seat in Fergus's armchair, leaving them to head to the study. It was time for Bex to find out why she'd been summoned back to Highland Hall.

13

As Bex walked away from Kieron, she was left with a peculiar feeling in her stomach. It felt like she had somehow offended him, and that wasn't what she wanted at all. She hadn't meant to feel like he'd been pushed out of the conversation or that she didn't want to include him, but this was business. Business and pleasure did not mix. She should've learned that lesson with Duncan, and Duncan hadn't been directly related to Fergus or the heir to this massive fortune. Even considering something as simple as friendship with Kieron felt like a big red flag at the moment, given everything she had to do. But then he'd been nothing but nice to her. Cooking her breakfast, asking her questions about her job. She would just have to tread carefully. Treat him as an employer as such. An attractive employer, who was undoubtedly attracted to her too.

'So,' Gordon said, taking a seat in the study, 'I expect you're wondering why Fergus wanted you here.'

'Yes. I thought you'd be able to deal with all this yourself,' Bex replied.

'Me too, to be honest. It's all very strange.' He adjusted his glasses and made a chewing motion with his lips. 'He sent several messages to me over the last couple of months, insisting that you attend to this, while he was clarifying his will.'

The word 'clarifying' caught in Bex's throat, causing a sudden weight of sadness to settle over her. Despite all the work he'd done around the village, and late-night whiskies, Fergus had known he was dying. Gordon nodded, as if he understood what she was thinking.

'To be honest, I think he got longer than he expected. Though, of course, he was too stubborn to let anyone know how bad the situation was. And I suspect the fact he kept going as long as he did led him to think that maybe things weren't as bad as he'd been told. But then... well, I'm sure you heard, it was a very sudden turn.'

'Yes, I did hear,' she said quietly.

So sudden that he'd not been able to get hold of Duncan, she thought, trying to push away the ache in her chest. Fergus hadn't wanted her up here to be sentimental. He'd wanted her here to do a job. And that was what she was going to focus on.

'Anyway.' Gordon coughed, clearly back in work mode. 'Your presence here isn't the only peculiar aspect of this estate.'

'No?' Bex asked. 'What else is it?'

Gordon sniffed slightly. 'Obviously, everything I show you in this room is confidential. And until we understand exactly what the implications are, we're not sure how to proceed. But here is the last will and testament of Lord Fergus McIntyre.'

He handed her the paper, though Bex hesitated to take it. Somehow, holding the document that contained Fergus's final wishes made it feel all the more real. It was silly, of course. There were no stages to death. Not really. Just before and after. But it felt like there should have been something more. Something to bridge that gap that felt so absurdly wide. The last time she had said goodbye to him had been no different to any other. She hadn't known that it would be her last visit to LochDarroch; she hadn't known Duncan would finally call the end to their relationship. She certainly hadn't known it would be the last time she would speak to the old man. If she had, she would have hugged him just a little longer. As unbelievable as it still felt, each interaction she'd had since arriving made it clearer that Fergus was truly gone.

Realising she couldn't leave Gordon sitting there with his hand outstretched forever, she reached out and took the document, at which point Gordon busied himself with his glasses, letting her read it in private.

As Bex scanned the first page, her professional instincts took over. She had read plenty of wills in her time. After all, inheritance law was her speciality. Though none had been quite as substantive an inheritance as this one. Still, the figures and bequests weren't what caught her eye, and as she turned to the second page, she realised what the issue was.

'My direct heir,' she said slowly, lifting her gaze and locking her eyes with Gordon. 'Kieron is not named.'

'No, he's not.'

'Why would he do that?' she asked. 'If Kieron is his only kin?'

'I dinnae ken,' Gordon admitted, his face solemn. 'But I was wonderin' if maybe, when you were lookin' through things, you found somethin' that might help make a wee more sense of it. If you had, it'd explain why he wanted you here.'

Bex shook her head. 'No. I don't think so.'

She continued to flick through the pages. There were names on the document, including his sister regarding sentimental items that had been handed down by their parents. But when it came to the largest endowments – the castle, the land, all the buildings and businesses in the village, even the dogs – it still said the same things.

'When was the will written?' she asked, thinking that perhaps if it had been before Kieron's birth then that would explain the name, though she seriously doubted that even Fergus would go thirty years without updating his will, and as she found the date on the front, she realised she was right.

'Under a year ago,' Gordon said, confirming what she had just read and dispelling that theory. With a long sigh, the lawyer removed his glasses and began to clean the frames on the bottom of his shirt.

'Well, we can't proceed until every avenue has been explored.'

Bex nodded. 'Kieron is not going to be happy about this,' she said.

'No, but if he's entitled to Fergus's inheritances then he'll get it in the end. It'll just take a little longer than expected.'

Bex handed the paper back to Gordon. What she had been shown had certainly proved this wasn't going to be a normal inheritance situation by any stretch of the imagination. But she still struggled to understand why he'd wanted her here. Unless it was like Gordon had said, and whether she knew it or not, something she had stumbled across in all the previous paperwork held the clues they needed to solve this puzzle.

Gordon looked at her as he slipped his glasses back onto his nose. 'I'm not sure why he's done this, but it would be chaos in the village if anyone finds out.'

'I can imagine,' Bex said. Screw the village. It would be chaos if Kieron alone found out. He had already introduced himself to her as the new laird and she couldn't imagine anyone would take too kindly to having something like that stripped from them.

'I can trust your discretion?' Gordon asked, the question implied in the rise of his tone.

'Of course,' Bex said, nodding as she still tried to make sense of what she'd just learned. 'I won't tell a soul. I just hope we work out what it means quickly.'

'You and me both,' Gordon said with a sigh. 'You and me both.'

14

Gordon and Bex remained in the study, where everything was exactly as she had left it, the only additions to the now organised piles of paperwork being the extra motes of dust that had settled on the surfaces.

'I put all the personal information that wasn't relevant to the accounting in there,' she said, pointing to a large dresser on the far side of the room. The glass cabinets and cupboards below were stacked with various notebooks, letters, even medical and vets' records, not to mention the occasional photo. More than once, Bex had asked Fergus if he wanted to go through it all and decide what he actually wanted to keep, but he had always brushed the suggestion off, saying it was something he would do later. Had he known then that he would never get a chance? Quite probably. Fergus hated paperwork. It was hardly going to be one of his deathbed wishes that he hadn't done more of it.

'Well, that sounds like a grand place to start,' Gordon said. 'We should probably get comfortable.'

They worked in near silence, only occasionally passing comment between one another as to whether something could be important. Yet in the quiet, Bex repeatedly found herself glancing around, looking for Ruby. The red lab loved nothing more than staying close to Bex while she worked, and strangely her absence felt almost more pointed than Fergus's. Hopefully, she would be able to see her a few more times before she left. Perhaps even persuade Duncan to let her take her for a walk. Not that it was great walking weather. Maybe she should try to convince Kieron to let the dog indoors instead. As a personal request. She wasn't sure if that would be easier or harder than convincing Duncan.

'Should've brought sandwiches,' Gordon said, a little after two. Four hours searching and they were no closer to discovering the reasons for Fergus's cryptic will. 'What do you say we pick this up tomorrow? I can give you a lift back to the village?'

Bex sat up straight, clicking her neck from side to side as she attempted to loosen her muscles.

'That sounds like a plan,' she replied. 'And a lift would be great. Thank you.'

Early January was a very different world compared to the summers in the Highlands. Just the walk from the front door to the car would leave her feet numb with cold, while deep grey, ominous clouds hung heavy in the distance. From the way the wind had bolstered since the morning, she wouldn't have been surprised if there was a storm on the way.

As she packed her things, Bex half-hoped she would see Kieron before leaving the castle, just to offer him a smile and ensure it didn't seem like they were conspiring against him, although now it actually felt a little like they might be. Either way, there was no sign of him. However, as she reached Gordon's car and went to open the passenger door, a distant voice cut through the quiet.

'Ruby! Esther! Come on, girls. Stop y' havering!' Duncan was calling for the dogs and so much of Bex wanted to go to him. To make sure he was okay, to tell him that she did still miss him, and to let him know that this was just as hard for her as it was for him. But he'd made up his mind and now putting as much distance between them as possible felt like the only kind thing to do.

When she arrived back at Lorna's cottage, Bex was officially done with paperwork for the day, which was why it was slightly unexpected to find the living room table covered in lists and notebooks, while Lorna was tapping away on her laptop.

'What's all this?' Bex asked with a sudden flurry of worry. 'Please don't tell me you're taking on another job. You really don't have the time for that.' Lorna was a chronic over worker, and coming from Bex, that was saying something.

'Not quite. Though it might lead to that.' Lorna shrugged before looking up from her computer. 'I'm doing some planning. Kieron messaged. He's having a Burns Night party. Wanted some help getting the village together.'

'Burns Night?' Bex questioned. She had heard of the celebration before. Apparently, back in the day, the Burns Night parties at the castle had been legendary. But the year before, she and Duncan had been down south visiting her family and Fergus had just wanted a quiet night. The year before that, she and Duncan had only been together for eight months or so, and though he'd suggested she went up, it hadn't fitted in with her work schedule. As such, she still wasn't exactly sure what it entailed.

'It's on the twenty-fifth. Celebrates Robert Burns. The poet,' Lorna told her. 'Anyway, Kieron's throwing one of his big bashes. Only he wants this one to be even more special than usual. You know, now that he's officially the laird and everything. He asked me to put together a list of people who we'd expect to come. Not to mention help with catering, cleaning. That kind of thing.'

'So, you know Kieron well?' Bex asked.

Lorna shrugged. 'Not really. Did a couple of wee jobs for him before. That's about it. I'm pretty sure he just asked me to do it because I was the first one he clapped eyes on this morning when he came in for a coffee.'

Bex pressed her lips together. Lorna was selling herself short again. She was massively talented, skilled and intelligent. Her problem was that she had so many talents, it was hard to pin down which path to take. One week, she'd talk about taking a business job, throwing her intelligence into spreadsheets and logistics. The next, she'd be focused on doing something crafty or artistic. Duncan had always worried about her, wishing she would decide on something and settle, but Bex loved her free spirit. It reminded her of her friend Daisy, who'd taken years to discover her calling was running a coffee shop on a canal boat.

'So, how did it go at the castle?' Lorna said as she closed her laptop lid. 'Any idea how long you're needed here yet?'

'Not exactly,' Bex replied. 'Looks like it's going to be a while, though. I suspect I'll still be here.'

'Right, what is it you're doing again?'

'Oh, just more accounting stuff,' Bex lied, careful to avoid her friend's eyes as she spoke. Gordon had warned her once again before they left that she was not to discuss the issue with anyone. But it was difficult. There was absolutely no one she could talk to about it, and it was such a big thing. The way Fergus had written his will implied there was another heir. There would be no other reason not to write Kieron's name otherwise. And Gordon seemed to agree.

'Well,' Lorna said, breaking the silence, 'do you want to go out for dinner? Or I've got some cheese in. I could make a rarebit if you fancy that.'

Bex raised an eyebrow.

'Cheese on toast?'

'Aye, cheese on toast,' Lorna replied cheerfully.

Bex rolled her shoulders. The stiffness from spending so long hunched over a table was refusing to shift. What she'd really love was a good massage, and no one gave better massages than Duncan. What she wouldn't give to have him work out those knots in her back. To push his thumbs deep into her muscles. She shook the thought from her head. Turning up on his door because she missed the dog and wanted her shoulders rubbed would give very mixed signals. The fact that she was still in love with him was irrelevant. Accepting that they had to move on was what mattered now.

'Cheese on toast sounds good,' Bex said. 'But I'll make it. I need to stand up for a bit. I feel like I've been hunched over bits of paper all day.'

'I'm not going to say no to someone making me food,' Lorna said. 'I'll nip in the shower while you're at it, if that's okay?'

'Sure thing.'

After changing out of her smart clothes into something far more comfortable, Bex went to the kitchen and opened the fridge. Unlike the one at the castle, Lorna's was well-stocked, though whether everything was still within its sell-by date was debatable. Still, after a little rummaging, Bex found some cheese and pulled out the chopping board. Then she opened the bread bin and found a fresh crusty loaf. She had just cut the first couple of slices when the doorbell rang.

'Lorna!' she called. 'Someone's at the door.'

The only reply Bex got was the sound of running water and, being fairly sure that Lorna wasn't going to suddenly leap out of the shower just so that she was the one to welcome her visitor, Bex set the knife down, brushed off her hands and headed to the door. She expected to find Niall, Eilidh or possibly both, as they were generally inseparable, despite their 'just best friends' situation. But when she opened the door, she found herself facing a man's back. A back, covered in a very expensive coat.

'Kieron?' she said.

Fergus's nephew turned to face her, the slightest crease folding the skin between his brows.

'Rebecca,' he said, a hint of a smile flickering on his lips. 'Can I come in?'

15

Bex wasn't sure why she was so taken aback by seeing Kieron there. Perhaps it was the abrupt way he'd turned his back on her at the castle and taken a seat in Fergus's chair. Or maybe it was just the unexpectedness of finding him in Lorna's little cottage when she was now wearing fluffy slippers, ready to make cheese on toast. Or maybe it had been the way he had said her name. Locking his eyes on her as he did.

An unexpected hot flush flashed through her as she cleared her throat.

'Lorna's in the shower at the minute. I can go get her. If you want to come in and wait?'

Of course he wanted to come and wait, she thought, cursing the stupidity of her question. It was bloody freezing outside. The only way he wouldn't want to come in was if he had some strange affinity with frostbite, and she was fairly certain no one in the world had that.

Though, rather than accepting her request, Kieron remained where he was.

'Actually, I didn't come here to speak to Lorna. I wanted to speak to you.'

'Oh.' Bex felt her jaw drop and hurried to bring it back up to its normal position. 'Okay, then. Yes, come in. Come in.' She stepped aside, letting Kieron into the cottage before closing the door behind him.

Kieron remained conspicuously silent as they walked down the hallway towards the living room. Once there, Bex wasn't sure if she should sit or stay standing. She felt too nervous to sit, but standing made her worry she'd shuffle her feet or start pacing, which wouldn't look good either. But why was she nervous? She hadn't been nervous while they had breakfast together this morning, but then maybe that was because she'd known why they were both there. She couldn't for the life of her fathom why he would want to speak to her now. Unless it was to ask what she and Gordon had been doing today. Yes, that made sense, but it didn't ease her nervousness. They had already decided that Gordon would field any questions from the potential future laird, but maybe he had tried that avenue and was now coming to her hoping to prise out more information.

'Can I get you a drink?' she asked. 'Tea? Coffee?'

'No, no, it's fine. I won't be long.'

'How did you find me?' she asked. 'Not that it's a problem. I just don't remember telling you I was staying here.'

'Right, of course. No, you didn't,' he said, stuttering slightly, as though he was as nervous as she felt. But why would that be? He was the one who had turned up here, after all. 'Lorna mentioned it when I bumped into her in the café today. She said you were staying with her.'

'Right, of course. That makes sense,' Bex said, nodding. 'She mentioned she'd seen you. She also said something about Burns Night.'

'Yes.' Kieron exhaled sharply before his eyes finally met hers. 'Look, I wanted to apologise to you about earlier.'

'Earlier?' Bex said, feigning innocence. But the quirk of his smile made it obvious he didn't buy it.

'I'm a bit of a control freak,' he admitted. 'I think it comes with my job. Or maybe I've always been that way. Mummy is somewhat of a wayward spirit. My father is much more measured, thank goodness, but being the only son and all...' He shook his head, letting the words fade into the ether. 'I don't want to bore you with my history or baggage. I just wanted to say I'm sorry for the way I reacted about not being included. It triggered some things for me, and that's silly because you were just doing your job. Gordon was just doing *his* job. And I was outright rude. I'm really sorry.'

'Oh.' Bex blinked, surprised by his openness. Not to mention the fact he called his mother Mummy still. 'Well, thank you. Apology accepted.'

As she spoke, a memory stirred in the back of her mind; Duncan, apologising after that disastrous night at the pub when his ex-girlfriend had shown up. She had been surprised then by how easily he'd owned up to his mistake, but it felt even more unexpected now, coming from someone like Kieron. London men didn't apologise that easily. At least, not the ones she'd dated.

'I get it,' she said. 'It must be a pretty stressful time for you.'

Kieron let out a light chuckle. 'That's one way of putting it. I've got the whole work thing to sort out. I mean, I should be back in London. It's the busiest time of the year for me, but...' He shook his head. 'Again, I don't want to bore you. I just wanted to apologise. And, since you already know about Burns Night, I wanted to invite you to join me. I don't know if you've ever been to one before?'

'No. No, I haven't,' she said. His eyes twinkled at her response.

'Well, you know what they say – you never forget your first.' As soon as the words left his mouth, he lifted his hand to his head. 'I'm sorry, that came out very wrong,' he said, though Bex expected that wasn't entirely true as the nerves she'd been feeling took a peculiar fluttering turn.

There was something between them – a spark, a moment. She hadn't been wrong in thinking he'd been interested in her at the airport, and that instant attraction hadn't faded. She was sure of it. And it wasn't like she hadn't found him attractive. He was every bit her go-to type when it came to city men.

For a split second, she was sure he was going to lean towards her, and her body was incredibly tempted to reciprocate the motion.

'Kieron? Is everything okay?' Bex turned to find Lorna standing in the doorway, one towel wrapped around her body, with another around her hair. 'I'm sorry, I didn't hear the door go.'

'It's no problem,' Kieron replied. 'I just came to see Rebecca.' He hesitated, then added, 'I wanted to... Well, it's about business.'

'You cannot turn up at her home just to make her do work, Kieron. That's ridiculous!' The indignation on Lorna's face was enough to cause a flutter of warmth in Bex. As was the motion of the cottage being her home, when she was in fact sleeping on a pull-out sofa for an undetermined length of time. But it was still very sweet.

'Don't worry,' Bex said quickly, feeling the need to come to his defence. 'It wasn't work exactly. Kieron also just invited me to Burns Night.'

'Oh.' Lorna's eyes widened. 'You're right, that's not work.' A glimmer shone in her eyes. 'Well, I assume you want to make sure Bex knows plenty of people there? I mean, she needs to be with her friends on her first Burns Night too, obviously.'

Kieron rolled his eyes, though the gesture was good-natured.

'I'm sure we've got room for a couple more,' he said. 'Just make sure you all dress appropriately.'

'As if I'd do anything but,' Lorna said with a grin.

'Well, I'd better get going,' Kieron said, turning back to Bex. 'Sorry about interrupting.'

'Honestly, it's not a problem. I'll walk you out.' She wasn't sure why she felt the need to do so. The front door really wasn't far away, but she wanted to.

'Thank you,' she said quietly. 'You know, for inviting Lorna and... thanks.'

'You're most welcome,' he replied, his voice soft as he stepped outside and a gust of wind blew in through the house, strong enough to rattle the pictures on the wall.

'Wow, you'd better get going,' Bex said. 'It feels like a storm's coming in.'

'Really?' He frowned. The winter evening had already drawn in, and outside it could have been midnight for all the light there was. 'It feels like an average winter night in Scotland to me,' he said with a chuckle.

But Bex recalled a night the year before, when the wind had been just like this, and she and Duncan had holed themselves up in the lodge while the winds howled and the snow fell.

'Trust me,' she said. 'When you've been up here enough, you get the feel of when a storm is coming.'

16

'Oh my God, I'm officially excited! I've always wanted to go to one of Kieron's parties.' Lorna was practically bouncing on the spot when Kieron left her cottage. 'This is amazing!'

'You haven't been before?' Bex asked, having assumed that when Lorna was putting the list together for village people to help Kieron out, she had included herself. Apparently, that wasn't the case. 'I thought he just invited the whole village.'

'It depends. When Fergus used to run Burns Night, it was just an open invitation. But it could get pretty chaotic. I went to a couple when I was a bairn, but then I used to babysit. Folk'd pay crazy rates. Like Hogmanay. Then Kieron started taking more control of them, and I think numbers were just too big to have everyone. You know, with his London friends and everything. There'd always be some people from the village. Kind of on a rotation. It's never been me, though. And some folk would always get an invite, like Moira. But now, Kieron has more of his fancy folk from down south. I guess he shows off the castle. I mean, it's great for the village, don't get me wrong. All the hotels are packed, the restaurants are bursting. But this year'll be amazing.

He'll want to have the biggest party ever now that he's officially laird.'

Bex felt a tightness squeeze around her throat, though she tried not to give anything away. She kept her smile perfectly in place when Lorna let out another screech.

'Oh! We're going to have to sort out dresses. And your tartan. I'm guessing you've not got any tartan?'

Bex raised her eyebrows. That was all she needed to do to convey her point. 'No,' she added, just for emphasis. 'I don't.'

'Okay, well, we'll go to Moira's one night this week,' Lorna said. 'Maybe if she's free.'

'To Moira's?'

Moira was the old woman who often sat in the corner of the pub with her knitting needles. The one with both infallible liver and eyesight. Though despite being a stalwart figure in the village, Bex had never really had any conversations with her one-on-one. She certainly wouldn't feel comfortable asking to borrow one of her tartans.

'Trust me, she'll love to help,' Lorna said, as if reading Bex's mind. 'Moira has the most insane collection of tartans. There'll be something perfect for you, I guarantee it. And maybe we should ask Eilidh about fixing a dress, too. I bet she could whip something up quickly.'

Eilidh was an incredible seamstress and textile artist, and Bex had no doubt that if she'd asked her friend in advance, she'd have loved to have made her something. But it was only eight days to Burns Night. There was no way she wanted to put her under that type of pressure.

'I'm sure I can just borrow something,' she said, trying not to dampen Lorna's spirit at the same time as making her see sense. 'Or order something online tonight. Otherwise, it sounds like quite a lot of effort for everyone to go to.'

'Of course it's a lot of effort. It's Burns Night at the castle! You're coming to your first Burns Night. At the castle!' Bex couldn't help but laugh. It didn't matter how much she wanted to be realistic about things, Lorna's enthusiasm was infectious.

'Let's just send Eilidh a message. See if she has any time before we get carried away,' Bex said, well aware that it was already way too late for that.

With a second shriek of glee, Lorna grabbed her hands and bounced up and down.

'Oh my God, this is amazing! Whatever you're doing to make Kieron like you this much, keep it going.' She grinned. 'I've always wanted to be invited.'

For a moment, Bex considered telling Lorna about her encounters with Kieron. Their conversations at the airport, when she hadn't known who he was, but they'd clearly been attracted to each other. She'd need to add that she'd walked away, though. She wasn't ready to even ask for a guy's number just yet. Not that she thought Lorna would judge her for that. Bex was single, after all, and Kieron was objectively gorgeous. But Lorna was Duncan's sister and deep down, Bex knew that she'd been hoping one day they would have moved from the position of friends to sisters-in-law. For a while she'd thought that might happen too. But now, that was never going to be. So what did it matter that she and Kieron had felt a physical attraction to one another, or they'd shared breakfast, or that the real reason he'd turned up on her doorstep was to apologise? It wasn't like anything was actually going to happen between them. No matter how much his damn eyes twinkled.

* * *

Several hours later, Lorna was in a bubble bath while Bex was on the phone to her mum.

'How's it going up there, darling? Have you seen you-know-who?' she asked.

You-know-who was obviously Duncan, and Bex wasn't entirely sure why her mother couldn't say his name. Probably because whenever she'd mentioned it in the last month or so, Bex had descended into tears. Thankfully, she didn't do that this time.

'Yes. Yes, we've spoken.'

'Spoken?' Mum picked up on the tone. 'What does that mean? Are you back together? Did you get into a fight? What happened?' From the rise in her mother's voice, Bex wasn't sure which of those things she would rather have happened.

'We spoke, Mum,' Bex said, deciding it was best not to go into how she had turned up at the pub when Duncan was flirting with Australians, then had to listen to him drunkenly rant about how he'd always known she would break his heart as she helped carry him home. 'Everything is fine. It's absolutely great.'

There was a pause, and she could picture her mum's expression: lips pressed tightly together, sucking her cheeks inwards.

'You know your father and I like Duncan very much—'

Bex gritted her teeth. 'Mum, I don't—'

'Just wait a minute. You don't know what I'm going to say. We like Duncan very much, and we know you loved him a lot. But you're a bright woman. If you knew that things weren't going to work between you, then you made the right choice.'

The tightness in her chest released by a fraction. 'Thank you, Mum. I appreciate that.'

'But of course, if you're up there and having all these doubts, then maybe you and him could have a talk. See if you can't work something out.'

Bex should've known her mother would be praying for a

reunion, just like half her friends were. Of all the boyfriends she had met, there had been none that her mum had loved quite as much as Duncan. And it wasn't just her mother. Bex's father and Duncan had got on brilliantly, too. Actually, everybody got on with him, which had made the whole situation so much harder. At least if one of them had been able to slag him off, and tell her what a good thing it was that he was out of her life, it would have made matters a little easier.

'That's not going to happen, Mum,' Bex said after a pause. 'It was a distance thing. You know that. And the distance problem hasn't gone away, just because I'm up here for a few days.' It was likely to be a lot longer than that, but she wasn't going to say as much. In her mother's mind, that would just be even more reason for her and Duncan to get back together.

'Well, if that's the case, then make sure you don't find someone else when you're up there.' Her mother chuckled. 'Let's be honest, they make some great men that side of the border.'

Bex didn't warrant the comment with a reply. Instead, her thoughts drifted involuntarily to Kieron. He might be up here in Scotland now, but he wouldn't stay that way, would he? It was difficult to know. Besides, thinking about Kieron in a dating manner was ridiculous, anyway. Yes, she had found him attractive and had considered asking for his number when they'd been at the airport when she hadn't known who he was. But she did know who he was now. And it wouldn't work.

'It's lovely to speak to you, Mum, but I think I probably need to head to bed soon,' Bex said. 'Got a pretty early start in the morning.'

'Oh yes. You still haven't explained to me what it is you're doing. I thought you sorted all the accounts last time you were there.'

Gordon had been very specific about not telling anybody

what was going on with the will situation, but it wasn't like Bex's mum was in regular conversation with anybody up in LochDarroch. And it would be so good to have somebody to talk things through with. She shifted over to the other side of the room, where she could hear the water continuing to run into the bath. Did that mean Lorna wasn't inside it yet? If that was the case, she could easily overhear.

'I'll explain when I get a chance,' she said, wishing she could tell her more. 'But like I said, I need to head to bed. Love you, Mum.'

'Love you to bits, Becky Boo. And don't work too hard.'

'As if.' Bex chuckled before hanging up the phone. Less than two days back in LochDarroch and life was already getting complicated. Fingers crossed it would be plain sailing from now on. Though something told her the chance was unlikely.

17

The next afternoon, Bex and Gordon were sitting in the study. They had spent the day going through all the paperwork they could find. Papers Bex had disregarded before because they were irrelevant to her accounting were now being scrutinised for any evidence of the 'direct heir'. Personal letters she had felt rude even scanning through were now being pawed over and dissected in hope of some hidden clue. But there was nothing.

'I've got a major sense of déjà vu,' Bex said as she picked up a small leather notebook and flicked it open to the first page. She stared at a list of hospital names, all of which had been crossed through, causing a memory to stir in the back of her mind.

Duncan had been helping her sort through the paperwork when he'd come across this one. The pair of them had made a deal: that if he helped her for five days – help which included bringing her lunch – then she would go on a date with him. Looking back at it now, Bex wondered if she'd already been falling for him then. This mild-mannered Scot who looked like he should be on some sort of topless calendar. She had fought it, naturally. Not only because she was there to work, but also because Duncan, in his recently broken-hearted state, was, in her opinion, undatable. Given how much they'd had to get through, and the absence of any financial data inside it, they had paid the notebook little mind, and had stacked it with all the hospital correspondence, which was exactly what she did again, before turning back to Gordon and letting out a groan.

'Part of me thinks that this could be his idea of a joke,' she said, rubbing her forehead. 'I can just imagine him, watching from wherever he is, laughing away.'

'Aye. Or...' Gordon said, removing his glasses only to leave the rest of his sentence hanging in the air.

'Or?' Bex pressed, not sure what Gordon had been going to say.

'Well, he was a generous man. A good friend to both of us, I reckon. Maybe it was his way o' makin' sure I could bill him for hundreds of bloody hours of work.'

'If that was the case, he could have just left us something in the will,' Bex countered.

'Aye, you're probably right,' Gordon said with a sigh. 'And the last thing we want tae do is get this wrong. I'm sure ye'd agree. If we let the laird's title go to the wrong person... I dinnae even know what the implications could be.'

Bex hummed as she contemplated the situation. Gordon was right. She had seen families torn apart over inheritances a fraction of the size of this one. But they had looked at all the known family members and one thing was certain: there wasn't an heir that was more direct than Kieron, so if there was an answer, she wasn't going to find it asking him.

As she sat there, mulling over the issue, Bex's phone buzzed with a text from Lorna.

Moira's. Tomorrow night. Sort out tartans.

Bex sent back a quick smiley-faced emoji and put the phone down.

A moment later, it buzzed again.

Do you have a black dress with you? Full-length?

No.

The next message came quickly.

No problem. I'll get Eilidh to make one.

Bex responded with a thumbs-up emoji, thinking that was the end of it. But the barrage continued.

You're a size twelve, right?

Yep.

Great. What sort of neckline do you want?

Gordon sighed heavily, cutting into her text exchange. 'Do you think you might want to just call her rather than let that ruddy thing beep all the time?'

He wasn't a grumpy man, but Bex could hardly blame him. The constant buzzing was annoying her, too.

'Sorry,' she said, quickly typing.

V-neck. Will speak later. I'm working.

She slipped her phone on to silent, placed it face down on the counter and moved across to Gordon. 'Sorry about that. What do you need me to do?'

Gordon removed his glasses. With the amount of time he

spent polishing his lenses, Bex couldn't help but wonder if he needed them at all. Or whether they were just some sort of stress-relief tool. He was certainly using them for that now. 'I think we might have to start looking beyond the study.'

'Beyond the study?' she echoed.

She had assumed, perhaps naïvely, that if they couldn't find the answer here among the masses of paperwork, that would be the end of it. Kieron would be marked as the heir, and they could all move on with their lives. She'd go back to London and away from the penetrating gazes of both Duncan and Kieron. But that didn't look like it was going to happen.

'There might be things in his room. Private safes, that sort of thing,' Gordon continued.

It made sense, but one thought nagged at her.

'Kieron isn't going to like that,' she said. 'How are you going to explain it to him?'

'Let me worry about the lad,' Gordon replied. 'We have to do what we have to do. Whether he's Fergus's nephew or not disnae change that he's nae the heir until we've gone through all this. He should know that.'

There was another option beyond the castle that Bex wasn't sure if she should mention or not. But if they were going to leave no stone unturned, then it made sense.

'Maybe after this, we need to start talking to people,' Bex said. 'People in the village. People who knew Fergus well. See if they know anything.'

Gordon raised an eyebrow. 'You'd think if folk knew there was another heir, they'd have said something, wouldnae they? And as for people knowing him, I didnae grow up in the village, but I'd known him a good forty years and would have considered myself among those tight with him, and I can tell you, this was as big a shock to me as it was to you. I don't think folk know anything more than we do.'

A long sigh escaped Bex. 'I'm not so sure,' she replied. 'People were very loyal to Fergus. You have no idea how long these things can stay hidden. I'm sure there are hundreds of secrets here that have gone to the grave with people. Maybe this was one of those Fergus decided, a little too late, that he didn't want buried.'

'If that's the case, I wish he'd been a bit more obvious about it,' Gordon muttered. 'I mean, if he had an heir, he could've just said it. He could have told me. He should've known I wouldnae judge him. No matter what the situation.'

That had to be it, Bex pondered. There was something to do with the situation that meant Fergus, for whatever reason, was too afraid to own up to it. A scandal of some sort. And possibly one big enough to rock the whole village if he was this desperate to keep it a secret.

Bex nodded. 'Do you mind if I take a break?' she asked, rubbing the back of her neck. 'I feel like I've been staring at bits of paper for hours.'

'Tell you what. Why don't we call it a day?'

'Really? It's only three o'clock.'

'I know, but I hate working when it's dark like this. No point scanning through things when we're tired. The worst thing would be missing something important because we weren't thinking properly.'

Bex agreed.

'Do you want a lift back to the village?' he asked.

'If that's okay?'

'Aye, it's always grand, lass. You dinnae have to ask.'

She climbed into the car and they drove towards the village.

It was less than a five-minute drive from the castle to the centre, but they chatted the entire journey. Although they hadn't been working together long, the pair had already learned a fair bit about one another.

Gordon had two grandchildren and was looking forward to retiring at the end of the year, though depending on how long this job went on, he was tempted to stop even sooner. He'd been married to his wife for forty-seven years, though she had turned down his first two proposals.

'Knew from the first day,' he had said once. 'First time I laid eyes on her, I knew she was the one for me. But she took a bit more convincin'. The second time I asked, I saw her waver. She was tempted. But I hadnae done it properly. So that's what I did the third time. I asked her da', got down on one knee, and the rest, as they say, is history.'

It was a sweet story. Forty-seven years of marriage was definitely something to aspire to, just like her parents' relationship.

'At the cottage?' Gordon said. Bex nodded and was about to thank him again when something made her stop.

Duncan was there, in the centre of the village, dressed in jeans and a thick coat, and just the sight of him was enough to make her throat tighten. She wanted to keep going until he was securely out of view, but before she could say as much to Gordon, her eyes shifted to the dog at Duncan's side. Ruby.

Ruby was Bex's favourite, but normally, whenever Duncan went for a walk, it was with all the dogs. Not just one. Then, with a stomach-clenching nausea, Bex realised they were standing outside the vet's office. Duncan had brought Ruby to the vet. Ruby was ill?

'Actually,' she said, turning to Gordon as her pulse rocketed, 'can you just drop me here?'

18

It was definitely Ruby that Bex wanted to see, Bex told herself as she hopped out of the car and walked towards the pair with her heart pounding. Definitely Ruby she wanted to check was all right, and not Duncan, who was standing there, brow furrowed with his hands plunged into his pocket as he chewed on his bottom lip. She hadn't seen that expression on him for a long time, but she knew what it meant. He was worried. And given that he was standing outside the vet's with her favourite dog on the lead, there only seemed to be one reason why.

'Duncan,' she said as she approached. 'What's going on? Is everything all right? Is Ruby okay?'

As he looked up, he let out a long sigh, and Bex couldn't tell if it was aimed at her. For a moment, she thought she was going to face the same Duncan as she'd helped home the other night. The one who blamed her for everything and would undoubtedly tell her to get lost. But then his gaze met hers and as he shook his head, she saw just how deep his worry went.

'I don't know.' There was a helplessness to his tone. 'She's not eating. I was hoping I could get someone to see her, but the vet's been called out to one of the farms. Looks like they'll be gone all night.'

The knot in her stomach tightened. A sick dog and no vet on hand. That was the problem with being somewhere like Loch-Darroch. There weren't exactly spare options if the person you wanted to see was busy. 'How long has she been off her food?' Bex asked.

'I don't know. She's no' been herself since Fergus—' He stopped himself. 'Since she came to me. And, you know, I thought it was, you know... missing him, but now that I think of it, she was pretty skinny when she came to me. Maybe she hasn't been eatin' properly for a while. I should have seen it.'

'You've had a lot going on,' Bex said, hoping he knew she meant it. The urge to tell him that whatever was going on with Ruby, not to mention how Fergus hadn't been able to get hold of him before he died, wasn't his fault was overwhelming, and she reached her hand out towards his arms, only to change her mind. Instead, she dropped to her knees and gently cradled the dog's head in one hand, while ruffling her ears with the other. 'What's going on with you?'

With the slightest sniff, Ruby wagged her tail hard on the ground, a faint glimmer of excitement showing through her malaise. Duncan was right. She was skinny. Even skinnier than Bex had thought when she'd seen her before.

'Huh,' Duncan said, letting out a huffing sound. 'That's the first time I've seen her wag her tail properly since I got her.'

'Really?' Bex asked, glancing up.

'Well, unless you include the other night,' he added.

'The other night? What happened then?' If they could work out what it was that made Ruby happy, then maybe they could work out what they needed to do to make her eat more.

Although rather than immediately replying, the tops of Duncan's ears turned pink.

'You helped Lorna bring me home,' he said. 'Bex, I'm so sorry, I didn't mean—'

A fresh wave of guilt flooded his expression and this time it was nothing to do with not noticing how ill Ruby looked.

'It's fine. Really. We all have nights we drink too much.' She kept her focus on Ruby, partly to assess how the dog was doing but also to avoid looking directly at Duncan. 'She's off her food, you said?'

'Yeah. Dry food, meat. She doesn't want any of it.'

'What about scrambled egg?' Bex suggested, finally looking back up at him. 'Have you tried her with that?'

'Scrambled egg?' Duncan's eyebrows rose. 'No, it's not something I feed the dogs.'

'Well, she loves it. She always did with me.'

Standing up, Bex glanced down the cobbled street. 'The café's still open,' she said. 'Why don't we get her some? My shout.'

Her heart pounded as Duncan chewed his bottom lip, considering her question for what felt like an eternity. Why had she asked him to go with her? She cursed herself. It sounded like she was asking him out for a meal, didn't it? And it wasn't like he needed to go to the café. She was sure he had plenty of eggs at home that he could use to whip the dog up a meal. So why had she suggested it? It wasn't because she wanted to spend time with him. It wasn't that every part of her body missed him so much it was painful, or that being this close to him, seeing him this upset and not being able to wrap her arms around him was pure torture. She was worried about Ruby and wanted to do all she could for her best canine friend. That was all it was. Still, her heart drummed as she waited for his answer.

Then, after what felt like the longest pause, Duncan dipped

his head in a nod and offered her the slightest flicker of a smile. 'Sounds good,' he said. 'But I'm paying.'

19

As Duncan and Bex walked into the café together, a familiar face stared at them from behind the counter. Bex saw the flash of disbelief radiating from her expression at the sight of the pair of them together, but within a heartbeat, it was gone.

'What's going on?' Lorna asked, directing her question at Duncan. 'Did you get to speak to the vet? Is everything all right?'

'They were out at one of the farms,' Duncan said. 'They won't be able to see her today.'

Bex should have known that Lorna knew her brother had been going to the vet's. She suspected, since the breakup, Lorna had known his every move, trying to stop him from falling off the rails. The thought caused a deep throb behind her sternum. It would be so easy to stop both their pain. To admit that they still loved each other and pretend the breakup had never happened. But what would be the point in that? So that a couple of months down the line, they would go through all this again, realising that when distance and lifestyle came into play, love just wasn't enough? No, they were better off this way.

'Could you get some scrambled egg, please, Lorna?' Bex

asked, refocusing her attention on the reason they had come into the café. 'It needs to be a big plate, but don't add too much milk to the eggs. Ruby doesn't like it with too much milk. But don't over-cook it either. She likes it a bit soft.'

Duncan's lips twisted into a smirk.

'What?' Bex said. 'You want her to eat it, don't you? That means it hasn't to be right.'

The smile glinted in his eyes. It was the first time she'd seen him look like that since she'd arrived in Scotland. 'You're ridicu-lous, you know that?'

'Says the man who took five dogs into his tiny lodge because he couldn't bear to see them sleep outside in a kennel.'

'Fair enough,' he replied with a shrug, although the smirk and glimmer disappeared and she found herself wishing she hadn't said anything.

It didn't take long for Lorna to bring out a plate of scrambled egg.

'We should give it a minute to cool,' Bex said, taking the plate and placing it down on the table in front of her. 'The last thing we want is her burning her mouth. She definitely won't eat anything then. Could you get us two caramel hot chocolates while we wait? Cream, marshmallows. The lot.'

'Sure.' Lorna's mouth twitched in a way Bex couldn't under-stand. Not until Lorna had walked away from them.

'Sorry,' she said, looking at Duncan and realising what she'd done. 'I should've asked. Are you okay with that? Having a drink?'

'Course. Been a long time since I've enjoyed one of those.'

The throbbing in her chest intensified as Bex realised what he meant. It had been impossible for him to enjoy hot chocolate since they'd broken up. It was the same for her. Hot chocolate had become a Scotland thing. Their thing. With Fergus some-times, too. Even though her best friend Daisy made excellent ones on her narrowboat in London, it hadn't felt right having one without him.

'This is probably cool enough,' Bex said as silence threatened to swallow them. 'Hopefully she'll have a couple of mouthfuls, at least.'

After blowing the steam from the top, and testing a forkful herself, Bex placed the plate of scrambled egg down on the floor in front of Ruby.

'Well, would you look at that?' Duncan said.

There had been no tentative sniffing. No deciding whether or not she could stomach it. Ruby was devouring the scrambled egg in great gulps, her tail wagging furiously as she did it.

'Should've known you'd have the answer,' Duncan said. Then, with a pensive look, he added, 'You know, come to think of it, I wonder if it wasn't Fergus she was missing after all.' He let out a sad chuckle. 'The way I see it, you've got two options. Either take her with you or never leave her again.'

The words caused a lump to rise in Bex's throat, and as her eyes met his, she knew he was only half talking about Ruby. Only it wasn't really an option, was it? She couldn't take him with her to London. Not forever. Not when his heart was so firmly here. And as for her never leaving, there was her job. Her job she had worked so hard for. Could she really just give that up? Then again, as she stared into Duncan's blue-green eyes, she couldn't help but wonder if it would be the worst thing in the world if she did.

As the lump in her throat refused to budge, and as the doorbell jingled announcing more customers to the café, Bex tried to find the words she needed. Words to make him understand that it had never been because she hadn't loved him. She had loved him so very much and she was pretty sure she still did.

Drawing in a shuddering breath, she opened her mouth, still not sure what she was going to say.

'Duncan.' Her voice cracked. His eyes were solely on hers. He knew, didn't he? He felt the same, right? She just had to tell him. 'Duncan, I need you to know that I—'

'Duncan! Oh my God, we thought we'd never see you again!'

The moment was broken by the high-pitched screech of voices that had come from the door and as Bex fought to regather her thoughts, she turned to find herself face to face with the two attractive Australians from the other night. This time it wasn't just Duncan's ears that turned fluorescent pink, but his entire face. 'Now you weren't ghosting us, were you, mate?'

'Sorry, ladies.' His Adam's apple bobbed visibly up and down as he swallowed. 'I've been pretty busy. Work. You know.'

'Well, we hear there's a big Burns Night party at the castle,' one of them said, smiling coyly. 'We're gonna try to scrounge some tickets... unless you know someone who can get us in.'

Duncan glanced at Bex, before turning back to them. 'No, sorry,' Duncan said firmly. 'I don't.'

They exchanged a look, clearly disappointed at not getting the reaction they wanted. One of them pouted dramatically, though in an instant, she was flashing Duncan a bright white smile. 'Fingers crossed, we'll see you around.'

'Right. Yeah.'

They moved across to the counter, leaving Bex and Duncan alone. The awkwardness of before was replaced by a whole different one. Duncan bit down on his lip, turning back to his hot chocolate. 'Sorry about that.'

'You don't need to apologise. You're moving on with your life,' Bex said.

He let out a dry laugh. 'No, I'm not. But I'm pretty sure you know that already.' He put his mug down, picked up a teaspoon and began to absentmindedly stir his drink. 'Guess you're just better than me at that, too. And, of course, you were the only person in the world who could make Ruby better. It just... sucks.'

Bex's chest tightened. Every bone in her body was screaming to tell him the truth, to tell him that she wasn't doing any better at all. That if you'd asked Daisy or Claire, they'd say she was just as much of a mess as he was. But how would that help?

'I might be here a little longer than I thought,' she said instead. 'There's some stuff at the castle... the will. It's not as simple as we'd hoped.'

Duncan's expression sharpened, his eyes narrowing.

'What? Why? I thought it would be straightforward. Kieron's the heir, isn't he?'

'Yes... of course,' Bex said quickly, realising her mistake. She'd promised Gordon she wouldn't mention this to anyone, and now, five minutes alone with Duncan, she'd nearly blurted everything out. 'Look, I'm sure it'll all be sorted soon. I'm not meant to say anything.'

'It's fine. My lips are sealed.'

Now that he'd mentioned his lips, Bex couldn't help but look at them. She felt herself drawn towards him, as if by some magnetic pull, but she stopped herself, pushing back from the table.

'Right, I'd better get home,' she said. She reached the door, but paused and turned back. 'I'm going to the Burns Night thing. I know what you said to those girls, but it'd be nice to see you at the castle.'

Duncan's cheeks drew inwards in what was almost as deep a pout as the Australian. 'Kieron invited you?'

'Yes,' she said. 'I thought... with all the work I'm doing there...'

'I don't tend to go to his things,' he said.

'I know. But it'd be nice to have another friendly face there.'

He nodded in response, but it was that type of nod that acknowledged he had heard what she'd said, rather than actually agreeing to show up. 'Let me know how Ruby gets on.'

As Bex looked down at Ruby's plate of scrambled egg, that had now been licked clean, Duncan let out a brief chuckle. 'You know, I wouldn't put it past the dog to pull this just to get us to spend some time together.'

Bex lifted her gaze to look at him, then smiled. 'Maybe,' she said, before looking back down at Ruby. If that was the case, then she wasn't sure if she should be happy with the dog or not. But at least she now had a reason to text Duncan again. If she wanted to, that was.

20

'You and Duncan looked like you were getting on well at the café,' Lorna said that evening.

'I think the word you're looking for is civil,' Bex said, although she felt a little bad saying that, so added, 'But it was nice to talk to him though. I just hope Ruby's all right.'

'Well, at least now he knows what to feed her. She might put on some weight.'

'I hope so,' Bex agreed. She was the one cooking tonight, though it wasn't very exciting. Pasta and pesto. It would fill a hole, and she didn't have the mental capacity for anything more. From the will to Duncan and now Ruby, there was a lot to worry about, and she was exhausted.

'And you're okay about tomorrow?' Lorna continued, grabbing the cutlery. 'About going to Moira's? Eilidh's already started working on your dress, and before you say she needn't have, she wanted to. She's just as excited as I am. It's going to be incredible. Oh, and don't think I didn't hear you invite Duncan along. Maybe a few drinks together is what you guys need.'

'Or maybe that is the worst possible idea ever,' Bex countered. 'And I didn't invite him. I asked if he was coming.'

'And said it would be nice to see him there.' She arched an eyebrow as she offered Bex a smirk.

'Exactly how much of the conversation were you listening in to?' Bex asked. 'Weren't you meant to be serving?'

'I can multitask. And I did very well.' Lorna's expression turned into a telling stare. 'I'll leave it. You know I will. I'm your friend as well as his sister. But honestly, seeing you talking like that, I just wanted to knock your heads together. You are the most perfect couple.'

It had been one thing hearing the same sentiment from Claire and Daisy for weeks on end, but it struck even harder coming from Lorna. Perhaps because she had been so forthright in warning Bex off Duncan when she'd first arrived.

'I get that it was difficult being together,' she continued. 'But was it really so difficult that it wasn't worth it?'

Bex made a slight hissing sound as she sucked in a breath through her teeth. Was it so difficult that it hadn't been worth it? It was hard to know the answer. They had coped as it was, but it would've just got harder, wouldn't it?

'I know you mean well,' Bex said with a sigh, 'but I really haven't got the energy to talk about this. However much he likes to pretend this is all on me, Duncan and I made a mutual decision.'

'He would have done whatever you said, and you know it. Besides, it doesn't mean you can't backtrack. It wasn't some legal thing, written in stone.'

Bex knew that, but she didn't say anything.

'Come on. Food's ready. Why don't you tell me more about Burns Night?'

* * *

The next morning, Bex tried to push thoughts of Duncan out of her head and focus on getting ready for work. Given the unpredictability of the weather, Lorna had given her a lift there every morning before heading to the café to start work. But as Bex stared out the window at the sun creeping over the horizon, she found herself fancying a walk outside.

Winter mornings in Scotland were like something out of a fairy tale. Crisp frost glittered on the grass and rooftops; smoke wove up from chimneys, filling the air with the scent of wood fires and homeliness. It was no wonder the village was constantly filled with tourists. Like the Australian women Bex was trying her hardest not to think of. Yet they were like pink elephants in her head. The more she tried not to think of them, the more the images, with their ludicrously long legs and perfectly manicured hands, took over.

It wasn't that she expected Duncan to call them again. They'd said it themselves – he'd ghosted them. But would he have done that if she hadn't shown up? And did she want him to, if it was stopping him from moving on, when they both so desperately needed to?

'Are you sure you don't want a lift?' Lorna asked as Bex pulled on her gloves. 'I really don't mind. I'm working the late shift at the café today.'

'Honestly, enjoy a lazy morning,' Bex said. 'I'll catch you later.'

'Well, don't be late,' Lorna reminded her. 'We need to see Moira. Remember.'

'I remember.' How the heck she thought she could forget, given the number of times Lorna had reminded her, was a mystery, but she didn't say as much. Instead, Bex wrapped her scarf tightly around her and headed outside. There was a nice coffee machine at the castle now, a gift Duncan had bought her before they were even together, which she'd left there for Fergus after they'd broken up. For Fergus, and because she didn't want to be reminded of just how sweet Duncan could be. Even now, when she looked at it, she would remember those early days. Moments like their first kiss, which had made her entire body melt.

As such, a desire for a takeaway coffee – rather than using the machine – was calling her. A hot drink would certainly warm her hands as she walked towards the castle. Not to mention delay how long it took to get there. Today, they really needed to start looking elsewhere in the house, and Bex wasn't sure if Gordon had approached Kieron about it yet. Part of her was happy to turn up a little later than usual, just so she wasn't there for the awkwardness of the conversation. But as she turned the corner to the café, she stopped.

Every muscle in her body begged her to turn around, but her feet were frozen. Bex had known that seeing Duncan would be hard, but now she realised there were going to be two other people even harder to face. Two people she had hoped, perhaps even prayed, that she wouldn't bump into, despite knowing the unlikeliness of that happening, given that she was staying at Lorna's. But by some miracle, she had managed it so far, and the lack of sightings had lulled her into complacency.

But there was no avoiding it now.

'Bex?' the woman said, her face breaking into a wide smile as she strode towards her. 'I'm so glad I got to see you. Heard you were back.'

'Carrie,' Bex said, an uncomfortable knot forming in her stomach as the woman engulfed her in a deep hug. Bex steeled herself for whatever was about to come. Like it or not, it was time she faced Duncan's stepmum.

21

Duncan's own mother had passed away when he was still very young, and Carrie and he were as close as Bex had ever seen a stepmother and son. Carrie thought of him as her own and saw all his qualities, not to mention all his faults. And she loved him unconditionally.

Like most people close to Duncan, she had been a bit wary when he had started a relationship with Bex, because of the issue of distance. But it hadn't taken her long at all to see that it was real love, and she had embraced Bex as part of the family. More than once, Bex had found herself thinking how Carrie and Duncan's dad, Keith, would've made perfect in-laws. And she was pretty sure they had thought the feeling was mutual.

As Carrie finally released Bex from a hug, she kept her hands on Bex's face and brushed a strand of hair behind her ear.

'Look at you. It feels like it's been forever,' she said.

'It's been a little while,' Bex admitted.

'How are you doing, darlin'? I'm guessing this hasn't been easy on you either. Have you been eating properly? You look like you've lost weight.'

'I'm doing all right,' Bex said, before reciting the words she must've said hundreds of times already. 'And it was for the best in the long run. You know, the distance and everything.'

Carrie's lips twisted, as if she could see through Bex with perfect clarity.

'Well, I'm sure the decision couldn't have been easy on either of you. And I know you two wouldn't have made it if you hadn't thought there was no other option.'

Bex smiled gratefully. It felt like the first time somebody had said that to her. Everybody else had just insisted on telling her how wrong she was. Or assumed it was all on her. Carrie hadn't done that.

'Getting a coffee?' Carrie asked, gesturing towards the café.

'Just before I walk down to the castle.'

Carrie nodded. 'I heard. Lots of hush-hush business going on there.'

Bex's eyes widened in surprise. She hadn't realised people thought what she was doing was secretive. Even though it was.

'Don't worry, I'm pals with Gordon's wife, Cary. I know she doesn't know what's going on either, so I'm not going to press you for any answers. You and Gordon'll let people know when you can. But I'd like to buy you a drink, for old times' sake, if that's all right?'

'That sounds lovely. Thank you.'

For the next ten minutes, Bex and Carrie skirted around the issue of her and Duncan's relationship and kept the conversation on far more neutral matters. How the village was coping with Fergus's death. When the funeral was likely to be. Not to mention Lorna, with her never-ending plans, and not quite living up to her potential. That kind of thing.

When Carrie had paid for both their drinks, they headed towards the door, but as Bex went to open it, she felt a hand on her arm. When she turned around, Carrie was looking at her with an expression of concern crinkling her face.

'You know, if you ever need me, as a friend, or as... I don't know what exactly,' Carrie said, 'but I'm always here to talk to you. You know that Keith and I thought the world of you, and that doesn't change just because you and Duncan didn't work out the way we all hoped.'

'Thank you. I'm really grateful. Honestly.' It was her turn to go in for a hug, and it left her wondering why she had been so worried about talking to Carrie in the first place.

'Take care of yourself, Bex,' Carrie said as they broke apart.

'I will.'

* * *

By the time Bex arrived back at the gate of the castle, the sun was casting yellow rays of light over the undulating hills. She had just finished her coffee, and was debating whether it would be wrong to get another straight away, when she spotted the figure standing outside the front door. He offered a small wave before walking over to her.

'Rebecca,' Kieron said, taking her by surprise as he kissed her on both cheeks. 'How are you doing?'

'I'm good, thank you,' she said.

'I'm so sorry I haven't been able to see you much of late,' he continued. 'I've been rather busy here now, with everything. Not to mention Burns Night. But you're okay, aren't you? You'll let me know if you need anything? I don't want you to think you can't ask me.'

It was a kind offer, considering how much he much he had going on.

'Of course, but I'm absolutely fine.' Bex glanced to her side, where Gordon's car was already parked. 'I see that Gordon's already here,' she said. What she really wanted to know was whether he had spoken to Kieron yet about looking around the rest of the house. From the slight pause, it seemed Kieron had.

'Yes, yes, he's been here.' He swallowed, lips pressing into the same position before he lowered his voice slightly. 'Between you and me, Bex, I'm not sure whether I should bring in some of my lawyer associates from London. You know, to help speed this up. I'm not saying that Gordon can't do the job, of course. I'm sure he was very capable once upon a time. But, you know, it's a colossal task, and maybe it might be a bit too much for the old chap.'

Bex felt a slight twist somewhere in her abdomen.

'I'm not sure,' she said. 'I mean, are you allowed to do that? Fergus appointed him, right? It's Fergus's estate. I mean, I don't know at all.' She let out a tight, slightly awkward laugh. 'Obviously I'm not a lawyer.'

'Right.' Kieron nodded, his eyes drifting off slightly. 'Wouldn't surprise me if my uncle made this as slow and difficult as possible. That was the type of man he was, as you're well aware.'

As he smiled at Bex, she felt her stomach tighten further.

Yes, Fergus certainly came across as grumpy and difficult, but that was only to those who didn't know him. The fact that Kieron still thought of him that way was a sign that perhaps he hadn't known his uncle as well as he thought. Or at all.

'I wanted to say thank you,' Kieron said. His tone shifted as his smile relaxed. 'I know that being cooped up in a stuffy old castle probably isn't your idea of great fun. Not to mention bunking down with the locals. You know, I'm sure your firm wouldn't mind paying for a room in the village.'

'I'm fine at Lorna's.' Bex meant the comment genuinely. Being on her own meant being in her own head, and that wasn't something she wanted at the minute. Particularly not up here. And the sofa bed was exceptionally comfortable. Now she knew how to set it up properly. 'And this place is hardly stuffy,' she said, quirking an eyebrow.

'You know what I mean.' He flashed her a grin, his twinkling eyes glimmering at her. 'You and I are city folk. The big smoke is in our blood. Like the damn loch water for these folks.' He sighed, broadcasting his arms around the area. 'Strange, you know. It doesn't matter how many holidays I spent up here, how much I tried to get to know the place, how many parties I try to throw for the locals. I'll never be one of them, you know. That's the thing with a place like this. Either you're a local, or you're an outsider. There's no in-between.'

Was he talking about her or himself? Bex couldn't quite tell. Something about his tone made her think it could be both. Bex's mind shifted back to Carrie. She had been born in America, and her thick accent remained, yet there was nobody more involved – or, as far as Bex could tell, beloved – in the village. Apart from perhaps Moira, of course.

'Anyway, it's good for me to know that you're there with Gordon,' Kieron continued. 'Fighting my corner for me.'

Fighting his corner? The choice of words caused a spike in Bex's pulse. Did he know about the will and how he wasn't necessarily going to inherit the laird's title, and everything else, for that matter? He was being very calm if he did. She parted her lips, not sure how she was going to find out, when he continued talking.

'I just mean, trying to get this sorted as quickly as possible,' he clarified, causing a wash of relief to flow through Bex.

'Well, everybody just wants to get this sorted as quickly as possible,' she said.

'You're right. Absolutely, of course. I didn't mean anything by it.' Kieron flashed her a smile, though it was replaced by a far more serious expression. 'Look, maybe, when we're back in London, you and I could get together under more enjoyable circumstances? If that's something you'd be up for.'

'More enjoyable circumstances?' she questioned.

'Dinner perhaps? Maybe a show?'

Was he asking her out on a date? Yes. She was sure he was. Dinner or a show didn't leave much room for misinterpretation. Besides, his eyes had that twinkle back in them, and like it or not, they really did cause a flutter in her abdomen, though she tried hurriedly to suppress it. How the hell was she meant to reply? It wasn't that she wanted to say no outright. There was a definite physical attraction, but was there more than that? It was hard to say. Then there was the minor detail of how she was also working for him. But if she said no, when she was still going to be here for an undisclosed amount of time, that would be more than a little awkward. And why would she say no, anyway? Because she still loved Duncan, who lived up here and would never move. Whereas Kieron had just said himself, he was a city boy. They were definitely a better match on paper.

'That would be lovely,' she said, before she could stop herself. 'When we're back in London.'

His smile broadened, taking that twinkle to a whole new level.

'I should get in, though. Gordon's waiting.'

'Of course, of course. Don't let me keep you.' He stepped aside, making room for Bex to step past, and as she just reached the door, he called out.

'Oh, by the way, I mentioned to some of my friends about the work you do. Friends who need accountants. There might be some good news for you there, too.'

'Well, thank you. I appreciate that,' Bex said, struck with an urge to get inside, which had nothing to do with the cold.

'No worries. Have a good day, Rebecca. See you soon.'

He left her with one of those flashing smiles, and she could feel something between excitement and nausea filling her. What the hell had she just agreed to?

22

'That's a lot of photo albums,' Bex said as she stared at the pile on the study floor. 'Where did you find these?'

'They were in the drawing room,' Gordon explained as he took a seat and dropped one of the heavy tomes onto his lap. 'Kieron wasn't too keen on me rummaging freely, but I noticed those when I was in there talking to him and it seemed like a good place to start. Before we go interrogating the village.'

'Did he not want to know why you wanted the photo albums?' Bex asked. Paperwork would be understandable, but photo albums seemed a little suspicious. At least to her.

'I said we'd found quite a few documents in the ones in here,' Gordon replied. 'Said his uncle had a strange form of filing. Said he didn't seem to know what kind of folders were for what.'

'You mean you lied?' Bex said, unable to resist a smirk.

'Aye, well, I prefer to say I was lenient with the truth,' Gordon replied. 'Now, let's see if there's anything that helps.'

Bex took another of the photo albums off the floor and randomly opened it up. Her heart did a sudden somersault at what she saw.

It was a picture of Duncan there with Fergus. Four dogs sat in front of them. None of the dogs were ones that Bex recognised, but that wasn't a surprise considering how old the image was. At a guess, Duncan was about seventeen. Around the age he'd been when he moved out of the family house and into the lodge, where he had lived with his parents before his mum's death. Bex remembered thinking it was sad that a boy that young would choose a life living by himself, rather than with the comfort of his family around him, but if this image was anything to go by, it had been a happy time. For both of them.

The pair of them were smiling broadly, with Duncan's arm slung over Fergus's shoulder, while the sunlight glinted off the loch behind them.

'Have you found anything?' Gordon asked, noticing the way she was staring.

Bex shook her head and turned the page. 'No. Just looking,' she said, before flicking through more of the images, searching for something to actually help them.

Most of the album seemed to have been given over to a village event, which included everything from traditional games, like caber toss and the hammer throw, to highland dancing, and an astronomical number of bagpipes. She stopped again to pause on what she was sure was a photo of a young Lorna, not to mention Horace and Roddy, who'd worked for Fergus.

'I think this one is probably too late,' she said after a few minutes, flicking through pages. 'If we're thinking that Fergus had a child, then it would've been before he married Winny, don't you think?'

While Bex knew Winny hadn't been the love of Fergus's life, that didn't mean he hadn't loved her. There had been a deep level of care and affection between the pair, who would have loved to have had their own children together. She couldn't imagine him having an affair. It just didn't seem like Fergus.

'I tend to agree.' Gordon nodded. 'So anything with Winny in it, we'll leave till later. Should help narrow things down.' He looked at the album in his hand. 'There's no sign of Winny in this one. If you want to look through, that is,' he said, handing her another album. 'I think most of these are earlier, actually.'

Having taken the album, Bex looked through it, flicking through several pages, until she found a photo that made her stop. She had seen it before, when she had sorted out all the accounts.

It was Fergus, Duncan's grandfather and a pretty young woman standing between them. While the image was in black and white, the woman appeared to have light blonde, perhaps strawberry blonde, hair. Her lips were thick, as were her eyebrows, while her cheeks were pushed into perfect rounds by the force of her smile. Bex had previously thought this woman could be the reason Duncan's grandfather and Fergus had fallen out. What if she had been spot-on? What if Fergus had loved her, and there had been a child involved?

'Do you know who this is?' Bex asked, showing Gordon the photo.

His jaw clicked as he pulled his glasses down to the end of his nose and studied the image for a moment before crinkling up his face.

'Can't say I do,' he said. 'Pretty face like that would have stuck in my memory for sure. She'd definitely left the village by the time I turned up. If she was from here.'

Was that good news? It was definitely a lead. One worth examining more.

'Do you mind if I take it?' she asked. 'I'm going to see Moira tonight. I can ask her. She might have some idea.'

'Sounds good,' Gordon said, nodding in agreement. 'Let's see how many more like that we can find. Someone's got to know something.'

23

Gordon had just dropped Bex outside Lorna's cottage when her phone rang. With her breath fogging in the cold air, she juggled her bag and her keys to open the door at the same time as answering the phone.

'Rebecca, glad I got hold of you.' Nigel's voice came down the line with its usual briskness. 'Is now a good time to talk?'

It would have been tempting to say no. After all, she and Gordon had already decided to call it a day – given how Gordon didn't like working once it was dark – and she had planned on having a long soak in the bath while Lorna was still at work. But it was only four fifteen, and she didn't want to admit to the drastically shortened working hours she had adopted since coming back up to LochDarroch. Although she doubted Nigel would have said much. He was a good boss like that.

'Sure,' she said, clicking the door behind her, well aware that was the only answer she could offer. 'What's up?'

'Well, I got your emails about this not being a quick job.'

'I know. I'm sorry.' Bex kicked off her shoes and moved into the living room. 'I know there's the Jenkins account to deal with, but Evan said he'd been able to cope with that.' Bex had already sent countless emails to various colleagues distributing her London workload while she was here. An advantage of being one of the bosses now. Even if she wasn't quite a top boss yet, she still had plenty of people to delegate to.

'Oh, don't worry about that,' Nigel said. 'Take as long as you need. If I'd known sending you up there would bring in this much business, I'd have had all my staff shipped out across the country.'

Bex frowned as she flicked on the kettle. 'Sorry, Nigel, I don't understand.'

'The company's acquired three new clients in the past two days. Big ones too. Very big. All recommendations with *your* name on them.'

She was used to people recommending her services now and then, but they had always been average-sized clients, if that. Never the sort to warrant this type of reaction from Nigel.

'Really? Are you sure?'

Nigel chuckled. 'They said they'd heard about what you're doing at the castle. Big estate work. Never knew there were so many folks who had places like that and needed our help. Let me tell you, Bex. People have noticed what you've done here. People at the top. The very top.' An excited flutter was building within her, but she was trying to keep a lid on it. After all, Nigel could just be ringing to say thank you. Not that she'd had anything to do with it.

'And that's good?' It all sounded positive, but sometimes it was hard to know.

'Put it this way. When you come back, that corner office is yours.'

'What?' Bex physically jolted as her heart clenched in her chest. 'Nigel, if you're messing me around...'

'I'm not,' he said firmly. 'I promise. It should've happened before. I got distracted. I'm sorry about that. But I'm serious now. The CEO's all signed off on it; that corner office is yours.'

Bex could feel her cheeks aching from smiling so hard as she propped herself up on the worktop, her legs suddenly struggling to hold her weight. This was what she'd been working towards all along, and now she had it. She'd finally got it.

Because of this job, she thought. No. She corrected herself. Because of the recommendations. It only took her a moment to work out who was behind them. Kieron, of course. He'd said he'd given the firm's name to friends who needed help, but she'd assumed he'd just made the comment in passing. She'd certainly never expected something to happen this quickly. First thing tomorrow, she was going to seek him out and thank him.

'This is amazing, Nigel,' she said aloud. 'Absolutely amazing. Thank you. Thank you for ringing me.'

'Pleasure's mine,' her boss said, in a way that made her think he was smiling too. 'Keep doing what you're doing up there, okay? Got any plans for the evening? I'm guessing it's not the ultimate nightlife in the Highlands.'

It took Bex a minute to realise he had asked her a question and was actually expecting an answer. Her mind was already in that corner office, having her choice of clients. Her choice of working hours. Her dream job. 'Sorry,' she said, coming back to the moment. 'No... not much nightlife, but actually, yes, I do have plans. Sort of. Clothes plans.' She was aware she was babbling, but it was hard to keep her thoughts straight. She needed to thank Kieron. As soon as possible.

'Well, enjoy them,' Nigel said, a finality to his tone, like he was ready to end the conversation. 'But don't get too comfy. You'll have to pick out furniture when you get back here.'

'Yes, yes,' Bex said, her pulse still hammering against her ribs. 'Absolutely.'

When she hung up, she continued to stand there, her pulse sky high, her cheeks burning from the constant grin on her face. Rebecca Barker. Junior director. She had done it.

24

Bex rang Daisy from the bath.

'A corner office,' she said, for what had to have been the third time at least. 'And a view of London. Well, maybe not of London exactly, more like the neighbouring office building, but still.' It was what she'd been working towards, what she'd dreamt of.

'You deserve it,' Daisy said. Given the obvious issue of Bex being in the bath, they were not on a video call, though Bex could tell from the clattering in the background that Daisy was packing up the coffee shop on her canal for the day. Again, Daisy wasn't normally one to finish work early, but Bex suspected it was to do with the weather. And it wasn't like she and Theo didn't make up for it in the summer. On hot days when the canal was particularly busy, they'd been known to keep it open for close to twelve hours. It was a dedication that Bex admired, though she knew what it was like when you loved what you were doing. Work just wasn't quite the same. Even if people never quite understood how anyone could love accounts and numbers the way that Bex did.

'So, have you seen any of Duncan since you helped him home drunk?' Daisy asked, taking Bex by surprise. Had she really not spoken to her best friend since then? No, probably not, given everything that had been going on.

'We went to the café together yesterday,' she said. 'It wasn't a planned catch-up or anything. Ruby wasn't very well. Actually, I should probably send him a message and ask how she's doing.'

'And that's definitely the only reason you want to message him, right?'

Bex didn't need to see her friend's face to know the smirk she was giving her. And hopefully Daisy would also be aware of the scowl that Bex returned.

'Yes, it is. He and I are... unworkable,' she said. 'And there's no point you or anyone else telling me what a shame it is. It doesn't change matters.'

A slight hissing sound came through the phone line, like Daisy was pursing her lips and trying not to say anything.

'You know best,' she said. 'So, tell me about the job. And what's the new laird like?'

It was Bex's turn to hiss slightly, not sure how the heck she was going to tell Daisy all there was to say about Kieron. Although Daisy misinterpreted the sound.

'That bad?' she asked.

'No, he's not bad, actually. He's the reason I got the job.'

'What? How?'

Bex knew she didn't have to fill Daisy in on all the details. Like the fact she had agreed to go on a date with Kieron when they were back in London. Or that she'd actually met him before. She could just tell her about him recommending her to his friends. Yet before she even gave her a scant outline, the doorbell rang.

'Crap. Sorry, someone's here. I'm going to have to go.'

'Okay, but you'll ring me soon, right? I want to know what's going on.'

'Course.' Water splashed out of the bath as she climbed out of it, her hair dripping wet, but not yet washed. 'Love you.'

'Love you too.'

A minute later, Bex was standing outside the bathroom with a towel wrapped around her.

'Who is it?' she asked.

'It's me.' Eilidh's voice drifted through from outside. Relief rushed through Bex. The last thing she wanted was Kieron or Duncan to see her half-clean and dressed in a towel. Bex opened the door, hit by a blast of freezing air as she let Eilidh in, then hastily closed the door behind her.

'Sorry, I guess I interrupted your bath,' Eilidh said, scanning Bex quickly up and down. 'Lorna said we should meet here before we go to Moira's. I guess she's still finishing up at the café.'

'Great.' Bex was aware that she was dripping water on the floor. 'You okay if I get finished up? Help yourself to a drink. Actually, there's some prosecco in the fridge if you want to open that. I'm in the mood for celebrating.'

'That sounds interesting.' Eilidh's smile lifted. 'Do I get to find out why?'

'Sure, just as soon as I'm dry and dressed.'

* * *

Fifteen minutes later, Bex's hair was only roughly dried, but it was clean and she was fully clothed as Eilidh handed her a glass of prosecco.

'So, what are we celebrating?' Eilidh asked. 'Are you and Duncan finally back together, or is it something to do with you and the future laird? I hear you two have been getting very close lately.'

'Where did you hear that?'

Eilidh offered a nonchalant shrug as she took a sip of her drink. 'Oh, you know what the village grapevine's like.'

Bex did, and she didn't like it. The last thing she needed was for it to get back to Duncan that she'd agreed to meet up with Kieron when they were back in London. Not that there'd been anyone there to overhear them speaking. No, whatever people were saying it was pure conjecture and nothing more.

'No, there's nothing going on with Kieron and me. Although, I suppose the celebration is *slightly* related to him. I've just been told I've got a big promotion at work. The big one. Junior director.'

She'd hoped the news would elicit a smile, and perhaps even a toast, but instead, Eilidh's lips twisted.

'What?' Bex asked.

'Oh, nothing,' Eilidh said, shaking her head and plastering the most fake smile Bex had ever seen on her face. 'Ignore me. Congratulations.'

She lifted her glass, for Bex to clink, but Bex left her drink where it was. Ignoring an expression like that was easier said than done. Not that she even tried.

'What is it? What are you not saying?'

'Oh, I don't know.' Eilidh avoided her eyes as she spoke. 'I'm just being silly. But I kind of thought that you coming back here, you and Duncan would reignite things. Then we'd have you here forever.'

Bex laughed, trying to suppress the ache that spread through her chest. 'You didn't really think that would happen, did you?'

'Oh, I absolutely did.'

Eilidh let out a sigh as she dropped down onto the sofa, at which point Bex followed. She didn't feel quite so like celebrating now after all.

'I know that's what everyone thinks should happen,' she said,

staring at the floor. 'But Duncan and I are complicated. It's not
that I don't love him. I adore him. But we have to think long term.'

'I don't mean to be awkward, but why? If it's love then it's
love.'

'We're adults,' Bex said, wishing she didn't have to explain
herself to people like this. 'We have to be practical.'

'That seems insane.'

'Really?' Bex didn't bother hiding her feelings as she lifted her
eyebrows so high they butted her hairline. 'As insane as being in
love with your best friend for a decade and doing nothing
about it?'

Eilidh's demeanour shifted immediately. Her jaw tightened.

'Niall and I are friends. Just friends.'

'But you're not,' Bex said. 'You're best friends. You call each
other all the time. You're each other's go-to person. He clearly
thinks you're gorgeous, and you get antsy anytime he mentions
going on a date with someone else.'

'I do not,' Eilidh snapped, before sinking back slightly. 'Okay,
maybe I do. But that's only because they're never good enough for
him. I'd be fine if he found someone that actually deserved him...
And are we now discussing *my* love life?' Eilidh shot back.

'Because mine's complicated and I don't want to get into it,'
Bex replied.

'And mine isn't complicated?' Eilidh shook her head. 'Niall
and I have been best friends since we were three years old. Taking
that chance... we could lose everything. The foundation of all our
memories could implode if it didn't work out. It's not worth that
risk.'

'And that's exactly what it's like with me and Duncan,' Bex
said. 'The chance of a happily ever after, of me finding a way to
make ends meet in this tiny village, isn't going to happen. And I
know Duncan would move to London if I asked him to, but I'd

never ask him. He'd hate it. This is where he's happy. And I can't give up everything I've spent my entire adult life working towards, because if I did, I'd end up resenting him.' She shook her head, unable to find the words to explain the hurt she knew it would cause. 'It's a lose-lose situation.'

Eilidh scratched her temple. 'It doesn't have to be,' she said. 'You could find a way, if that's what you really want.'

'Well, maybe that's the answer, isn't it?' Bex said. 'Maybe we don't want it enough.'

Yet, as the words left her mouth, a dull ache throbbed behind her sternum. Was that the problem? Did she not love Duncan as much as she'd convinced herself she did? Or did she love him so much that she'd got out before she ended up irrevocably broken?

The silence between them stretched, neither willing to speak first. For a moment, Bex feared they'd sit there forever until the front door clicked open.

'Hey, guys!' Lorna said as she stepped into the living room. 'Oh great, we're drinking already. I'll grab a glass. Who's ready to sort out outfits?'

Bex and Eilidh exchanged a quick look, the tension of their previous conversation still fizzing around them. Yet with a slight nod, they silently agreed that now was not the time to continue the conversation.

'Sure.' Bex smiled at Lorna as she grabbed the bottle of prosecco. 'It sounds like just the type of distraction we need.'

25

Moira lived in a detached, whitewashed house at the far end of the village. Loch View Cottage was what the sign on the gate said. And the loch view part made sense, but as for cottage? It was at least three times bigger than Lorna's place, and plenty big enough for a large family home, though as far as Bex was aware, Moira lived on her own. She couldn't imagine why one woman would need so much space. Although, as she pushed open the gate and stepped inside, the thought was superseded by another.

'Damn,' she muttered to herself, stopping on the path so abruptly that Lorna almost went into the back of her.

'What is it? Everything okay?'

'I had some things I wanted to ask Moira about. Some photos I wanted to show her,' Bex replied. After the phone calls with Nigel and Daisy, and then the conversation with Eilidh, she had entirely forgotten to bring them.

'Photos? Of what?' Eilidh said, the lilt of her voice indicating she was clearly keen to know more, although the question made Bex nervous. There was no way she could tell her the truth. Not without giving away the issue with the will. So maybe it was better that she hadn't brought the photos at all.

'Oh, just of her. I think. When she was younger,' Bex said, both grateful and embarrassed at how easily the lie had slipped from her lips. 'I was going to ask her if she wanted them.'

'That's so sweet of you, Bex.' Lorna reached out and squeezed her hand. 'I'm sure she'll appreciate them whenever you can drop them over.'

'Right. Yes, of course. You're right.' Bex forced a smile to her lips. At some point, when all this came out, her friends would have to learn about everything she'd been keeping from them. Then again, if Kieron did turn out to be the direct heir, maybe none of it would come out at all.

Wanting to change conversation as quickly as possible, she raised her hand to knock on the door, though it swung open before her knuckles had even hit the wood.

'Come away in. Y'll freeze tae death out there.'

Bex had only ever seen Moira sitting down before. Always in the corner of the pub, and always with a knitting needle or crochet hook in hand. She didn't even get up to go to the bar – Bex was fairly sure that she never bought her own drinks anyway – and as such, the sight of her standing upright caused a jolt of surprise. Bex had never assumed she was a big woman, but she also hadn't realised she was quite so tiny. The old woman, with her grey hair and thick woollen clothes, couldn't have even reached five feet, yet that didn't stop the force behind her words. 'Quick, will ye? I dinnae want the cauld rushin' in. And tak your shoon off. I dinnae want you draggin' dirt in.'

Bex did as she was asked, hurriedly removing her shoes and coat, before following the others further into the house.

'Right, find yourself a seat,' Moira said in her thick, lilting accent. 'I'll be a tick.'

'This is insane,' Bex said, wide-eyed, as she took in their surroundings, suddenly understanding why Moira needed so much room. It wasn't a house. It was a haberdashery. A craft shop. A shrine to all forms of arts, crafts and knitworks. From where Bex was standing, she could see three different types of sewing machine, along with another large white machine with several metal prongs that could have been a torture device, but which she assumed was for knitting or sewing or something similar. There was even enough room to hold classes.

'I know,' Eilidh replied, her voice dripping with envy. 'Look at all these fabrics, threads and laces. And this is only half of it – it all goes upstairs too.'

To the left of the window was a large cabinet filled with different types of yarn, the kind Bex had seen Moira knitting with in the pub, while various half-finished projects were draped over the back of chairs.

'When my mum realised I liked sewing, she got Moira to give me lessons,' Eilidh said. 'Before her arthritis, that woman could whip up a full ballgown in the blink of an eye. Incredible.'

'But we're not planning on wearing ballgowns to Burns Night, are we?' Bex asked. Since sending Lorna the message about her size, she'd not even thought about her dress. Surely Eilidh hadn't made her a ballgown?

'No. No ballgowns,' Eilidh said. 'I've got your dress in my bag. Bear in mind, it definitely needs some work doing on it. Alterations and things. You should probably try it on before we go looking at tartans.'

'Okay,' Bex replied, happy to do whatever her friends told her.

'You can get changed next door,' Eilidh said, with an authority that told Bex she had been here plenty of times before. 'Just yell if you need help.'

The room Eilidh had sent her to had a full-length mirror in, and even though the dress was a bit baggy, and the sleeves weren't finished, Bex could already tell it was going to look fabulous.

Back in the main living area, Moira nodded her approval. 'Grand, so it is,' she said with a wrinkled smile. 'Right then. Let's find a tartan tae go wi' it. What colours dae ye like?'

'Maybe something red?' Eilidh suggested.

'I'm more of a blue person,' Bex said.

'Blue? Well, there's a nice one from Glen Orchy. Oh, or the Fife tartan has a lovely blue.' Moira shuffled around and headed over to a large blanket box beneath one of the sewing machines.

'You do know all the tartans are from different districts, don't you?' Lorna said as she fingered through a pile of silk fabrics.

Bex raised an eyebrow. 'Are they? I never really thought about it.'

'Folk usually wear the tartan of their district,' Moira explained. 'But nae one's gonna mind if you wear something different.'

Moira rummaged through a stack and pulled out a vibrant red tartan. 'This is the Fife. What do you think?'

Bex slung it over her shoulder, but hesitated. It wasn't that it wasn't pretty. It just wasn't quite right. 'Do you have something purple?' she asked, suddenly keen to see another colour.

'Purple?' Moira's eyes lit up. 'Oh, the Longniddry tartan. Now *that's* special. Real special. Let me dig it out for ye.'

After a quick search, she brought out a beautiful tartan in shades of purple and light blue.

'That's absolutely gorgeous,' Bex said, running her fingers over the fabric.

'Well, go for this yin,' Moira said, a nostalgic smile on her face. 'Unless you've got a reason nae to. I'll tell you something about it. I wore this to my first Burns Night at the castle.'

'You did?'

'Aye, I did,' Moira said proudly. 'Oh, it was a special day. This is where I'm from. Longniddry. It's a little village just east of Edinburgh. I came here as a nervous young thing, just eighteen years old, and got invited to the castle. Fergus...' She trailed off, her expression softening. 'Well, Fergus was a young man then. Very bonnie. Fancied myself a bit of that, I did. Of course, he only ever had eyes for—' She stopped abruptly and visibly swallowed before trying to smile, but it was too tight to be believable. 'Ignore me. Just an auld woman haverin'.'

Bex glanced towards Lorna and Eilidh, who were busy looking through more fabric while lost in conversation.

'You knew,' Bex said, trying to stop the way her heart was hammering in her chest. 'You knew the other woman? The one he was in love with before he married Winny.'

Moira's eyes narrowed as they fixed on Bex. 'How do you know about that?'

'He told me,' Bex said. 'Well, not much. Just that his marriage to Winny was more of a convenience, and that he had loved someone else. He said she passed away before he got a chance to propose. He said he didn't even get to say goodbye.'

Moira's gaze remained sharp. 'That's very strange,' she murmured. 'He must've thought an awful lot of you to confide in you like that. It was a long time ago. Not sure anyone in the village remembers it. Anyway, that's nae something we talk about.'

'Moira...' Bex's pulse was continuing to rise, though her voice was a near whisper. 'There's something I need to ask you. Something we think happened with Fergus and this woman.'

Moira's jaw locked, and any trace of her smile was gone. 'Like I said, that isnae something we talk about.'

'But it's—'

'Take your tartan, lass,' Moira cut her off as she handed the tartan to Bex before speaking loud enough that Eilidh and Lorna could hear, drawing an end to the evening. 'And have a braw time at the castle. Now, you should probably get off. You've got everything ye need frae me.'

26

The wind was biting as Bex and the others made their way back through the village to Lorna's. Every day since her return to Scotland, she had been certain they were going to be hit with a snowstorm. The type where even a walk to the café was a near impossibility. She had even said as much to Kieron when he'd come to the cottage, but so far, the heavy snow had evaded them. Fingers crossed they wouldn't have a whiteout on Burns Night. That would hardly seem fair, given all the work Kieron and everyone else were putting into the event. But having a massive celebration at the end of January in a part of the country known for temperamental weather was bound to cause problems now and then.

'You okay? You're pretty quiet,' Lorna said as she opened the front door. 'Were you thinking about how hot you're going to look in your dress and how Duncan and Kieron aren't going to be able to take their eyes off you?'

Bex groaned and rolled her eyes.

'No, I was just thinking about work. That's all.'

That was one way of putting it. What she'd really been

thinking about was Moira's response and the way she had closed up completely when Bex had tried to push her for more information. She knew who the love of Fergus's life was and probably a lot more gossip too. If anybody was going to help them with their problem, then Moira was almost certainly the woman they needed. But Bex and Gordon would have to convince her to help without making it feel like she was betraying Fergus. Which she wouldn't be, of course. This was what Fergus wanted, after all. He wanted everything to go to his rightful heir. Maybe they would just have to show her the will. She would suggest as much to Gordon in the morning.

'I'll get your dress ready for Tuesday,' Eilidh said as she took the bag back from Bex, bringing her out of her thoughts. 'And sorry about earlier, you know, when things got a little... tense.'

'What happened?' Lorna asked. 'Why did things get tense?'

'Oh, nothing,' Bex said quickly, shaking her head. 'We were just offering our opinions on different matters, that's all.'

'Oh.' From the bluntness of Lorna's tone, she knew exactly where the friends' differing opinions lay. Thankfully, she didn't say any more.

'You don't have anything to apologise for,' Bex said, hoping Eilidh knew how much she meant it. 'I know you only care. And I'm sorry too. I pushed that matter way too far. And thank you for the dress. It's stunning. You are amazingly talented, you know that. When you become a massively famous clothes designer and need an accountant, don't forget about me, will you?'

'It's a deal.'

The pair squeezed each other in the type of hug that could only be shared by friends who knew that, no matter what, they were there for each other. Arguments would happen, but the friendship would stay.

'Well,' Lorna said with a grin, 'now that's sorted, I fancy a drink. Do you want to come to the pub? We could celebrate. You know, a toast to finding the perfect tartan?'

Bex laughed. Lorna's ability to make everything into a celebration was almost as skilled as her ability to bring Bex's love life into every conversation.

'I'm in,' Eilidh said. 'Though I don't want a late one. Seeing all those fabrics has given me the inspiration for some new designs, and I want to get some sketches done before I go to bed. And I need to finish Bex's dress. Though don't worry, I'll do that sober tomorrow,' she added, with a glance at Bex.

'We'll just go for one,' Lorna said, and Bex couldn't help but wonder if she already knew that was a lie.

'Bex?' Eilidh said. 'Are you coming? We still need to have a proper celebration for your new promotion?'

'Right, yes,' Bex mumbled. Somehow, she had forgotten all about the corner office that would be waiting for her when she got back to London.

'I would,' she said, already knowing what the girls' response was going to be. 'But I've got so much work to do tomorrow. It's probably best if I get an early night. Besides, I'm guessing Tuesday's going to be a big one.'

The smirk on Lorna's face said it all. 'Oh, it's going to be a very big one. A *very* big one. You should probably give your liver a warm-up by having a couple of drinks tonight.'

Bex narrowed her eyes. 'I'm not sure that's how it works. Actually, I think that's the opposite of how it works.'

'It's fine,' Eilidh said, placing a hand on her shoulder. 'You have an early night. I'll see you soon.'

'See you soon,' Bex replied.

Five minutes later, the girls had gone, and Bex was on her own, though somehow she knew an early night wasn't going to happen.

For over an hour, she stared at the selection of photos she had taken from the study, but she kept coming back to the same one. The one with Duncan's grandfather and the woman between him and Fergus. There was no denying the way the men looked at her. They loved her. Both of them. She was sure of it. Yet neither of them had ended up with her. She had died before Fergus had a chance to propose. Duncan's grandfather, Bex already knew, had disappeared for several months, then returned to LochDarroch with a woman no one knew and a newborn baby. Possibly a response to losing the love of his life, too?

She studied the woman. Why did it feel like there was something familiar about her? Was it just because she wanted there to be? Right now, her head going around in circles, wasn't helping at all. Tomorrow she would talk to Gordon and they would speak to Moira together. And this time they wouldn't take no for an answer.

The next morning, Lorna was in no fit state to drive Bex to the castle. Unsurprisingly, one drink had meant starting with one bottle of wine between the pair of them, then one shot, then one of whatever they fancied or someone gave them. Lorna had come in at two singing and wanting to teach Bex highland dancing. Insistent was a nice way of putting it, and it had taken a fair amount of persuasion for Bex to convince Lorna that while she would like to learn at some point, it wasn't the right time. Finally Lorna had relented and headed to her bedroom where, within a matter of seconds, she was snoring and was still doing so when Bex got up and dressed several hours later.

Lorna had said on countless occasions that Bex could borrow her car, but it didn't feel right. Not when she was passed out and unable to tell Bex if she needed it or not. As such, she was walking to the castle again.

The temperature had definitely dropped, and swirls of snow were drifting down from dense grey clouds that entirely obscured the sun. Still, it was a light enough flurry that barely settled on her coat as she made her way down the path towards the castle.

Her first instinct was to make a coffee and warm up her hands, but given how Gordon's car was already parked outside, she headed past the study first to see if he wanted one, too. Inside, Gordon was already seated in an armchair, not a scrap of paper in his hands. And considering it was only just gone nine, he appeared absolutely defeated. His skin was grey, and he looked like he hadn't had a good night's sleep in days. Given how this task of theirs could well go on for months, Bex couldn't help but think that perhaps Kieron had been right in suggesting that Gordon wasn't up to the task. Or at least that he needed to bring someone else in to help. She would do what she could, of course, but she wasn't a lawyer. It was still a mystery to her why Fergus had even wanted her here.

'I'm grand,' he said, noting the way Bex was looking at him. 'Honestly, just been dealing with a lot of questions, you know.'

'From Kieron?' Bex guessed.

'Aye. Wants to know exactly what the hold-up is and why he hasn't been able to see the will yet. Threatened to get his own lawyers up here, like I don't know what I'm doing.'

Bex bit down on her lip. Perhaps suggesting he needed to get extra help wasn't a good idea after all.

'Well, I spoke to Moira last night,' Bex said, wishing she could give him a little more positive news. 'I didn't take the photos, but she knows who the other woman Fergus was in a relationship with was.' Gordon's eyes widened. 'She didn't give me a name, but she knows it. I'm sure. I think we need to tell her about the will.'

His lips pursed. 'I'll have to draw something up for her to sign. You know, so that she can't mention it to anyone.'

'Right,' Bex said. Legal implications like that hadn't even crossed her mind.

'Come on,' Gordon said, adjusting his glasses as he stood up. 'I've had my wallow. We should get on. The last thing I need is the so-called laird poking his head around the door and thinking I'm not working.'

'Would you mind if I leave you to it for a minute?' she asked, still standing in the doorway. 'I was going to make a coffee. And I need to go talk to Kieron about something.'

Gordon's eyes flicked up to meet hers.

'Should I be worried?'

'Not at all. It's about London. I'll be back in a minute,' she added quickly placing her bag down on the floor. 'I just need to thank him for something.'

'Okay,' Gordon said, returning to his work. 'Oh, and we're out of coffee pods. Sorry. I used the last one before I realised.'

'No worries,' Bex said, trying to look like she meant it. Any workday without coffee was tough, but one where Lorna had had her up at 2 a.m. was a different matter entirely. She'd have to work something out if she was going to make it until the afternoon.

* * *

Like Fergus, Kieron had taken to spending his days in the drawing room. He had even moved a small desk in there to work at, and she couldn't help but wonder if it had been a less than subtle hint that he wanted her and Gordon out of the study, or ideally, the castle, as soon as possible. Though, however brusque he'd been with Gordon, he'd been nothing but polite to her. And now, with this new promotion, she really did owe him.

She had just reached the grandfather clock in the hallway when the front door of the castle opened. A gust of cold air blew inwards and before she realised what was happening, a red blur came bounding towards her and leapt up at her legs.

'Oh my goodness, look at you!' Bex said as she crouched down. 'You look like a different dog!'

She ruffled the dog's belly as it rolled onto its back, her tail thumping on the floor as her tongue flopped out of her mouth. Bex's cheeks ached as a wide grin and with a slight move of her hand up towards Ruby's neck, she located the dog's favourite place for a scratch. The tail wagging reached a whole new level. As did Bex's grin. She knew she'd missed Ruby, of course. She'd often thought of the dog when she woke up at night, her room notably empty, and not just because of Duncan. But she hadn't realised she'd missed her this much. Happy tears pricked her eyes as she prepared to bury her face in the dog fur when a throat cleared above her.

'She just wanted to come and tell you she's feeling better,' he said.

With one more rub of her fur, Bex rose to her feet and found herself face to face with Duncan.

'Is that right?' she asked, still unable to stop her smiling.

'It really is,' he replied. 'We started walking past the castle, and she began barking. So I had a suspicion you were here. You were right. The eggs worked wonders. I mean, I guess it's not too much effort, just cooking extra for her in the morning.'

'Look at you,' Bex said, beaming at the dog. 'I'm so glad you're feeling better. I was worried about you.'

She was about to crouch back down when Duncan spoke again.

'So you're working here again today?' he said. 'You must have a lot to do. I hope it's going all right. And staying with Lorna is okay, I hope? I hear she had a bit of a late one last night? Hope she didn't disturb you too much?' There was something about his tone. The multiple questions. As though he were searching for something to say. A reason to stay there talking to her.

She shrugged. 'It's all good, thank you. Busy.'

'Right. Okay. Well, if you've got a lot to do, I should probably leave you to it.'

'I do have a lot to do,' she admitted, wishing her responses hadn't been so blunt. She wanted to talk to him. Though what they had to say, she wasn't sure. She wasn't sure if she even needed to *talk* to him, or just being like this, near him, was enough.

'What is that animal doing inside?'

Bex snatched her gaze away from Duncan to find Kieron standing there, looking at Ruby with a mixture of disbelief and disgust on his face, though even when his eyes moved to Duncan, his expression remained the same.

'Sorry, this is my fault. Not Duncan's,' Bex said.

'Really, I find that hard to believe,' Kieron muttered. 'She's not your dog, is she?'

'No,' Bex admitted. 'But we have a special bond, from when I was here before. And she wasn't feeling very well when I saw her the other day, and I was worried about her. She just wanted to say hello. Show me that she was better.'

'She started barking when we passed the house,' Duncan added. 'An inseparable pair. That's what they were.'

There was something about the way Duncan's eyes shifted to Bex that told her he was no longer talking about her and Ruby, and it caused her stomach to tighten.

'Is that right?' Kieron asked, raising an eyebrow.

'Yes, yes. Inseparable,' Bex replied, not sure if she was talking about Duncan or Ruby, either.

Silence swirled around the three of them, awkward and almost incomprehensible. Bex knew she had to break it, but she wasn't quite sure what to say. Somehow, though, after clearing her throat and forcing a smile to her lips, she managed to find the words.

'Well, thank you for bringing her to see me. I really appreciate it,' she said, looking at Duncan, before twisting around to speak to Kieron. 'Do you have five minutes? I was hoping I could talk to you about something.'

A slight smile lifted Kieron's mouth. 'You should know, I always have time for you, Rebecca,' he said, gesturing towards the drawing room. 'Come on in. I've just put some logs on the fire.'

Kieron turned and walked a few steps, but hesitated at the doorway and turned back.

'Unless you need something else, Duncan?' he asked. 'I assume the animals can be removed from my home now?'

It was only when Duncan flashed Bex a final smile, then turned and left the castle, that Bex realised Kieron had said animals, not animal. Did he think Duncan had brought another dog into the house? No, she realised with a pang of guilt. That probably hadn't been it at all.

As always, the drawing room was wonderful, warm; the fireplace had probably been lit constantly for the past thirty years – it had certainly never been out whenever Bex had been in here. But despite being its normal temperature, Kieron had made several changes to the space, including moving Fergus's chair. Bex tried not to dwell on the matter as she followed Kieron inside.

'Sorry if I was a little rude out there,' he said, an expression of remorse flicking on his face. 'It's just a lot to get to grips with, you know. Boundaries with the staff, that kind of thing. I guess it's trickier to navigate than I'd expected.'

Bex had never once heard Fergus talk about anyone who worked for him as 'staff'. In fact, she would have bet her new corner office that he knew the first and last names of every person who worked for him, but it was probably wrong to expect the same of Kieron. Until now, he had been in and out of this world so sporadically. And he was obviously trying. 'Now, come. Sit down. I'd offer you something to drink, but I just headed downstairs and we're out of coffee. I'll make sure we've got plenty in tomorrow. Although...' He offered the slightest flicker of a grin. 'If you'd like to have this conversation over something stronger, maybe later tonight, I'd be happy to oblige?'

The line could have sounded cheesy. A blatant chat-up line, but there was something about Kieron that was effortlessly charming. Was it a boarding school thing? she wondered. He'd told her he went to boarding school, so perhaps it came from that. Or maybe it was just natural charm. She'd certainly worked with well-educated people who had no concept of basic manners, but Kieron wasn't one of them. Not when he was speaking to her anyway.

'My boss, Nigel, rang me yesterday,' she said, making it clear the conversation was going to happen now.

'I hope there aren't any issues?' His eyes widened, as if the question was genuine. Was he not aware of what had happened?

'Not at all. He wanted to thank me for all the extra business I've brought his way. Though, obviously, it was business *you* brought his way. I assume you are the reason he had so many people give him my name?'

'Oh?' There it was again; definite surprise. Although it quickly transformed into a smile accompanied by that twinkle in his eye. There was no way someone could learn to do something like that. No, that was pure charm alone. 'Well, I'm glad I could help. Like I said, you've done such a great job for me. I really appreciate it. Actually, I'll be rather disappointed when everything is finalised. I'm not sure what the castle's going to be like without you here.'

He held her gaze with an intensity that caused her mouth to dry. 'We've still got plenty of things to sort out before we leave.' Bex tried to keep her tone neutral, not wanting to say anything that might hint at the complications they were facing with Fergus's will. 'We could be here a little while longer.'

'Well, I'm not going to complain if that keeps you a little closer.' She swallowed hard. While the room was notoriously warm,
she wasn't sure that all the heat was coming from the fireplace.
'And I should probably tell you that I wasn't aware your boss was
going to ring you at all. Or that I'd actually succeeded in getting
you more clients. I sent out a WhatsApp message to some friends
in London. To be honest, I didn't know if any of them would
contact the firm, but I'm glad they did. You deserve it.'

'Thank you.' How did she keep finding herself looking into
his eyes? Bex wondered as she was once again drawn to those
deep irises. Although from the way he was looking at her, it felt
like a mutual issue.

'Well, I should probably admit my actions weren't entirely
altruistic.' Before explaining what he meant, he stood up, walked
over to the mantelpiece and picked up a folded piece of paper.
'This was in my pocket when I got here. It was actually still in my
pocket when you walked in and accused me of sitting in Fergus's
chair. I couldn't decide whether to burn it or give it to you. I am
still not entirely sure this is the right thing to do. But here.'

He held out the paper, which Bex realised was actually an
airline napkin. When she unfolded it, she found his name and
number written inside.

'I spent the whole flight debating whether to ask one of the
air hostesses to give it to you,' he said. 'But I chickened out. Then
I thought I might see you when we landed, and I actually hung
around for a little, but... well, I decided that was kind of creepy to
have a man you'd barely had two conversations with loitering at
an airport hoping to speak to you again. So I got in a cab, figured
that if I was meant to see you again, fate would play its part. Well,
that was what I thought for about fifteen minutes, until I
completely regretted my decision and wished I'd marched up the

plane and asked you out then and there. When you came in here the next morning...' He let out a trembling breath as he took another step towards her. 'When you walked in here, shouting at me for sitting in the armchair, there was a reason I kept my back to you for so long; I just didn't want to believe it was real. That I'd actually found you again. It feels like fate, doesn't it?'

Heat rose in Bex's chest, spreading upward. He was a gorgeous specimen of a man who wasn't intimidated by her own career or ambition. Who clearly respected her for who she was. Wasn't that what she had spent years looking for, before... before... She wouldn't let the rest of that thought form. 'It was certainly a very strange coincidence,' she said carefully. Kieron took another step towards her.

'When I came to Lorna's the other day to invite you to Burns Night, it didn't quite go as planned. I wasn't just asking you as an employee or even as a friend. I was asking you to come with me. As my date.'

The words rang in her ears.

He wanted her as his date. Kieron, possible future laird of Highland Hall, wanted *her*, an average accountant, to be his date at the first official event at the castle since Fergus's death.

'Wow,' Bex said, the word slipping out before she could stop herself.

A pink hue coloured Kieron's cheeks. 'I apologise. I've caught you off guard, haven't I?'

'No! No. Well, actually... yes, completely.' She laughed nervously. 'Thank you, though.'

'Hmm.' A crooked smile played on his lips. 'Is that, "thank you, I'd absolutely love to attend as your date" or "thank you, but that's not an offer I'm going to accept"? It's fine either way, obviously.'

Bex looked down at the napkin in her hand, the inked number staring back at her. Why the hell was her pulse so fast? It wasn't like it was the first time a man had asked her out.

'I actually considered doing something similar,' she admitted. 'Well, not sending a napkin, but, at the airport, I was hoping you would be there when I got off the plane.'

'So is that a yes?' His eyebrow rose, as did his smile. And Bex wanted nothing more than to say yes, just because it felt like the right thing to do. But that wasn't a good enough reason to go on a date with someone, was it? Particularly not a date that would be as public as this one.

She hesitated. 'Things are a little complicated for me at the moment.'

'Complicated?' His smile fell by a fraction.

'I'm just out of a serious relationship.'

'Oh, I'm sorry. I assume it's not anybody I know?' There was no hint of irony in his voice, and Bex realised that he had somehow missed it all. The tense moment in the kitchen when they'd been having breakfast and Duncan had shown up to get dog food. And only moments ago, outside with Ruby. Kieron hadn't noticed how they had struggled to be together. How their hearts were still in tatters from the knowledge that they would never work together, regardless of how much they loved one another. Bex's stomach tightened.

'No.' She flashed a smile as she lied. 'Someone back in London.'

'Right.' Kieron nodded, before drawing in a long breath. 'Well, that's good to know. And there's no pressure. You don't have to decide right now. I won't rescind the offer and I certainly won't be inviting anyone else. But if you want to stand with me, it would be nice to have a dance or two.'

'A dance or two sounds nice,' she said softly, before standing up a little taller and clearing her throat. 'Well, I should get back to Gordon. He'll be wondering what I've been doing all this time. Thank you, Kieron.'

With that, she turned around and walked out of the drawing room, wondering why the hell she had lied about Duncan and if her heartbeat was ever going to return to a normal pace again.

Bex felt somewhat dazed as she ambled out of the drawing room. There was a pounding behind her temples that could have come from a lack of coffee, but could also have come from everything she was trying to juggle in her head. From keeping the will a secret, to Kieron asking her out, to the fact that she had lied about Duncan when she had been presented with the perfect opportunity to say exactly who she was heartbroken over.

Why did it matter if Kieron knew that she and Duncan had been a thing? Their dislike was certainly long-rooted, but was that purely because he thought of Duncan as staff? That was a him thing, not a her thing. She knew exactly who Duncan was; the type of man who brought a dog by the castle so she could see she was doing all right. The type of person who had loved her with his whole heart, but ultimately blamed her for the demise of their relationship because he had been too blind to see that if they'd kept going the way they had, they would have ended up hating each other.

'Gordon, I just need to go out for a quick walk,' she called down the hallway. She couldn't deal with being in the study, looking through papers again, trying to unravel Fergus's past when she couldn't even do that for herself. Not when her chest felt like it was going to explode.

Desperate for some fresh air, she didn't even bother going and getting her bag from the study. Instead, she grabbed her coat from the stand, pushed open the door and stepped outside. The air was even more biting than it had been an hour ago, and the shroud of grey cloud seemed to be hanging even lower in the sky. Yet she paid it little mind as she picked up her pace and walked away from the castle.

Her initial plan had been to head up to the village and get a coffee, then go to the shop and get some more coffee pods to ensure the caffeine withdrawal didn't happen again. But as the cold air flooded her senses, she found herself craving something other than caffeine. She needed space to think. Real space. And despite having been back in LochDarroch for five days, she still hadn't been to the loch. That was what she needed. She needed to see the water, clear her head, and make sense of whatever was going on in that messed-up head of hers.

As she took the narrow path down towards the water, Bex's mind continued to whirr. What was she doing? Why was she doing this?

She liked Kieron. She'd liked him from the very first moment she met him. He was charming, intelligent, respectful, kind, and undoubtedly wealthy. He ticked every box of what women were looking for. She'd be insane to turn that down, wouldn't she? Yes. But that didn't change the fact that nearly three months after their breakup, her heart was still well and truly taken.

Ex-boyfriend in London? London, like hell.

There was only one person muddling up her brain like this, and she hated him for it. Her mind filled with the image of Duncan, flirting with those girls at the bar. What would've happened if she hadn't appeared in the pub? She shook her head, trying to push the thought away. She already knew. They would've gone back to the girls' suite, presumably. How many times had he done that, thinking it didn't matter? Thinking she wouldn't find out? Thinking what she didn't know couldn't hurt her? But then, why *did* it hurt her? Why did it make her feel like she couldn't breathe?

They weren't together, and she had explained to every person who'd asked why that was the best thing. Why they wouldn't work long term. But then she hadn't gone on a single date since they had broken up and now, when a guy made it very explicit that he wanted to get to know her more, she was freaking out. Was it because, like Eilidh had said, she thought somewhere along the line it would work out between her and Duncan? That they would find each other again, when the moment was right? When fate intervened? But Duncan didn't believe in fate. Understandably, given how he had grown up. Kieron did, though. Kieron seemed to think her showing up like this was the universe telling him she was meant to be in his life. It was hard to deny that the chances of them being on the same flight and then here together in the same castle in this tiny village were more than a little unlikely. If fate was real, then surely Kieron was the person it was drawing her to?

Unlike the morning, the flakes of snow seemed to be settling, yet she stumbled onwards, pulling her coat tighter as the wind kicked up a notch.

Across the field, on the other side of the woods, Bex spotted a small contraption. The clay trap. Her heart clenched. Though it hadn't been an official date, Duncan had taken her there when they'd gone for their first walk together. He'd explained to her about clay pigeon shooting and showed her what she needed to do, then he'd held his chest up against her back and he'd wrapped his arms around hers, then guided her fingers over hers as they pulled the trigger together. She could still feel the warmth of his breath on her neck, his body pressed into hers.

What would it feel like if it were Kieron's body pressed up against her instead? Did she want to know how it felt to have his arms wrapped around her? She wasn't sure. And what about if it erased everything she had felt with Duncan; would she want it to? Surely the answer was no, but if it took away the pain of thinking of Duncan with those other women, then that was another matter entirely.

She wasn't running so much as fast walking now, and not towards the trap. No, she had been wrong to think she should come here when the memories were almost as catastrophic as the castle. What she needed was to get to the village. She needed to get to the village, get a drink and call her friends. They would help her make sense of it all. They would tell her she was just panicking about nothing. That this was what happened when you started dating again after being in a relationship. But as she turned around, looking, she found herself struggling to know what direction to head in. She wasn't sure when it had happened, but the snow had fallen so swiftly, she could barely make out her footprints. And it wasn't helping that it kept drifting in her eyes. Every time she stopped to wipe it out, she found herself more and more disorientated.

'Sort yourself out, Bex,' she said, not sure if she was talking about her heart or her navigational skills. She knew this loch. This land. She and Ruby had spent hours walking here. Sometimes with Duncan or Fergus, but sometimes just on their own. And not once had she ever got lost. This was not going to be the first time.

Determined to work out where she was, she kept walking forward, searching for something familiar, but it wasn't just the snow that was stopping her from finding her way. Her breaths were growing shallower and the wind howled as it bolstered to such a force she struggled to stay on the path she had set for herself, while a deep fog drew in so quickly that soon, she could barely see two feet in front of her. It was with a terrifying nausea that chilled all the way to her already freezing bones that Bex finally realised the truth.

She was out in the Highlands, in the middle of a storm, with no idea how to find shelter.

30

Bex screamed until her voice was hoarse. Turning in circles, she yelled out for someone to help her. To hear her. To save her. More than once, she tried walking desperately, hoping that she might stumble across a place to shelter. An old forgotten cabin. A den or just a hollowed-out tree trunk. But there was nothing but barren earth and snow-covered rocks. And soon she could barely hear her own cries above the screeching wind, let alone expect anybody else to.

Tears stung Bex's cheeks as they met the freezing air. She was soaked to the bone, shivering in a way she had never shivered before. And she was lost. Utterly lost.

She pictured the headlines now: *London Woman Tragically Dies in Highland Snowstorm*. There would be pictures of her smiling, articles mentioning how she had spent some time in the area and naïvely thought she'd known it. Then all the safety awareness warnings would follow. There would be emergency numbers to call when you got lost. Apps like what3words. Duncan had told her about it before. How the developers had designed a system where any location in the world could be identified by three words and she knew it had already saved countless lives, from people who had got injured out on remote walks to kayakers who had got in trouble out on the water.

Duncan had insisted she upload the app onto her own phone in case of an emergency like this. And she had. Even when she'd moved back to London, she'd left it on. Only her phone, and any chance of help, was back at the castle.

'Help! Anyone!' Bex cried again as she wrapped her arms around herself, trying to stop the chattering of her jaw. She couldn't die out here. Not like this. She couldn't. This wasn't how her story ended. She had too many chapters left to write. Too many adventures and experiences left to have.

But it was so cold. Every inhale made her shudder more and more, and the cold was searing through her feet. Every step was agony.

Deciding that perhaps preserving her strength was the best thing she could do, she stumbled on towards a thin tree trunk. Then, with a sound close to a whimper, she lowered herself to the ground and pulled her knees into her chest as her back pressed against the rough bark.

Why was it so hard to keep her eyes open? Was it because of the cold, or was it because of the disturbed sleep? Maybe that was it. Maybe if she just closed her eyes and let her body rest for a minute, she would find the extra energy she needed to start walking again. And if the storm passed quickly, then maybe she could see the castle and climb her way back.

She needed to get back to the castle. She had to. There were so many things she needed to say. To people. To her family. To her friends. But most of all, to Duncan. She needed to speak to Duncan and make sure he knew it wasn't because she didn't love him. She loved him. She would always love him.

As she swallowed back tears that filled her throat, Bex closed her eyes, wishing she could feel herself folded up in his arms one more time. The cold didn't feel so bad all of a sudden. She hardly noticed it. Instead, numbness had taken over her body.

Maybe if she just went to sleep, then she'd wake up when the storm was over. Sleep would be the best way for her body to recover. She would move after sleeping.

As her eyes remained closed, Bex thought how, in the distance, she might have heard people calling her name. But surely it was her mind playing tricks on her. Just like the dog barks she could hear. Barks that sounded just like Ruby.

Ruby, she thought, a warmth spreading through her chest. Ruby was a good dog. Maybe Duncan was right. Maybe she should adopt her after all. But maybe now she wouldn't get the chance.

As Bex's body threatened to slump to the side, she felt something warm hit her. Warm and wet. She straightened up, wanting to reach out and take hold of it, to grasp the warmth. But she wasn't strong enough.

'It's okay, I'm okay,' she whispered, not even sure who she was talking to. The cold was almost gone now. And this warmth she had found was so incredibly comforting. She would have happily stayed there and slept forever. Only as that thought struck, she felt the pressure of arms around her body, scooping her up out of the snow. Strong arms that held her in place as the voice spoke.

'It's okay. You're okay. I've got you now. I've found you, Rebecca. You're safe now.'

31

The first thing Bex noticed was the pressure on her feet. Unfathomable heavy pressure. She tried to shuffle them, to flex her ankles or just wiggle her toes a little, but they wouldn't move. She couldn't move her feet.

Panic rose through her as the memories snapped into place. The storm. She remembered going out and getting caught in the snowstorm. She'd been freezing. She had been freezing and lost and had known there was no way out of there. Oh God, was it frostbite? It had to be. With a surge of terror, she tried to roll to her side, expecting the rest of her body to resist. To perhaps be unable to move, like her feet, but instead the pressure beneath her ankles suddenly subsided, and she flopped sideways. Her whole body felt free, including her feet. They still ached, but they were definitely moving. Her toes too. Painful, but wiggling, none-theless.

Utterly disorientated, she was still blinking open her eyes when she was ambushed by a wet, slobbery lick across her face.

'Ruby,' she said, wrapping her arms around the dog and

burying her head in the dog's fur. 'Oh my goodness. I am so glad to see you. I'm so glad to see you.'

She could feel the tears stinging her eyes against skin already raw and bitten by the ice and snow. How was she okay? How was she here? And where was here exactly? She had so many questions she needed answers to, though at that moment, all she wanted to do was hold her dog as close as possible.

'That dog of yours is probably the reason you're alive,' said a voice.

She tilted her head up to see Kieron standing at the side of the bed. Her bed. Or at least it had been when she had first come up to LochDarroch. This was the room Fergus had given her to stay in. She was back at the castle. But how?

'The storm,' she said, the memories coming in bits and pieces. 'It came in so fast.'

Kieron nodded. 'But why had you gone out in it in the first place?'

She shook her head, not sure she could give an answer that justified what a complete fool she had been. 'I was just going for a walk. Clearing my head.'

Pain flashed across his face. 'Because of what I said? Rebecca, I'm so sorry if that's the case. If I came on too strong. I would never... I could never...'

As Kieron's words drifted into silence, Ruby moved again, so close that Bex was practically spooning the dog, and somewhere in the recesses of her mind, she vaguely remembered feeling something warm and wet before she passed out completely.

'You said Ruby's the reason I'm alive,' she said suddenly. 'How did you find me?'

Rather than replying immediately, Kieron smoothed down the quilt and perched on the edge of the bed. 'When the storm came in,

Gordon came and found me. He said he thought he heard you yell something about going for a walk but wasn't sure. Anyway, when you didn't come back, we got worried and went outside where we bumped into the groundskeeper. I hear you know him quite well.'

It was with a pang of guilt that Bex remembered what she had said to Kieron, about her ex being a guy back in London. Clearly, she had been busted for that.

But Duncan. She remembered thinking about Duncan just before she thought she was going to die. All the things she had wanted to say to him, though now, she struggled to remember what they were. Or how she would even face him after making such a foolish mistake.

'Yes,' she said in response to Kieron's comment. 'Yes. We were...'

She didn't finish the sentence, and from the way Kieron's lips pressed together, she didn't need to.

'Well, he was coming up to the castle, and the dog was going berserk. Once it had got our attention, well then we just followed it.'

The tears that had stung her face only moments ago were now rolling freely down her cheeks. 'Thank you,' she said weakly, before turning back to Ruby. 'And thank you, too. Thank you so much. You're such a good dog, aren't you? You are such a good dog. Yes, you are.'

As she nuzzled into the animal once more, she realised she was no longer dressed in her own clothes but instead a set of flannel pyjamas. The type of which she had never seen before.

With a flush of heat rising to her cheek, she looked back to Kieron.

'Are these... yours?' she asked.

He nodded. 'Yes. Duncan was the one to put you in them, though. You know, to preserve your dignity and everything.'

It was clearly not a conversation he wanted to have and to be fair, neither did she. So she said something else instead.

'I thought you didn't like animals as pets,' she said, gesturing down to Ruby. 'And certainly not on the bed.'

A smile flickered on Kieron's lips and, for the first time since she had seen him standing there, that twinkle returned to his eyes. 'Well, I thought an exception could be made for this one. After all, I'm not sure I'd have found you without her. You gave us a hell of a scare.'

'I scared myself a bit,' she admitted.

His eyes locked on to her. 'You've no idea how glad I am to see you okay,' he whispered.

A lump filled Bex's throat as she nodded in response, only now realising that his hand was resting on hers.

Hurriedly, she pulled it away. 'I'm so sorry. I don't even know what time it is. I've wasted so much of your day. I should get going. Get dressed. Get to work. Get... Get...' She wasn't exactly sure what she should be doing, other than not sitting in the large double bed in Kieron's pyjamas staring into his eyes as he held her hand. Yet as she pushed Ruby to the side and went to stand, the blood rushed from her head. It wasn't just dizziness; her whole body felt woozy.

With her heart racing, she dropped back onto the bed.

'You're not going anywhere for a while yet,' Kieron said firmly. 'You're staying exactly where you are. Let me get you something to drink. And as for work, we're putting whatever it is you and Gordon are doing on hold for the foreseeable future.'

Bex didn't have the strength to argue. Instead, she nodded, then sank herself down into the pillow as Ruby nestled back beside her.

Ruby had saved her. Ruby was the reason she was alive.

As Bex slung her arm back over her dog, she let out a yawn.

Her eyelids were heavy again. Desperate to close. But the sound of voices in the corridor caused them to ping open.

'I heard you talking to her. If she's awake, I need to see her. Now.' It was Duncan's voice. Her heart fluttered. Duncan was out there.

'She needs to rest,' Kieron replied.

'I need to see her. I swear to God, Kieron, either you move out of my way, or—'

'It's fine,' Bex called out, pushing herself back up. 'It's okay, Kieron. Let him in.'

A moment later, the door opened, and Duncan stepped inside. His whole face was grey and sallow. Though she wouldn't have thought it possible, he looked worse than when she had first arrived at the castle.

A feeling rose through her as she remembered the minutes before she had passed out. The desperate need to tell him, just one more time, that she loved him. To let him know, in no uncertain terms, that he was the love of her life and if there was a way, any way, that they could work it out between them, then they had to try. She knew it now. She knew without a doubt. That was why Fergus had wanted her to come back here, because he'd not wanted them to go through what he'd gone through, losing his one true love. Not when there was no need for that to happen.

But as she opened her mouth, ready to say it all, Duncan's expression changed. A thundercloud rolled across his face as harsh and cold as the snow that had fallen outside.

'How the hell could you be so stupid?' he yelled.

All the words Bex had been feeling only moments ago were swallowed into the ether. She had seen Duncan angry before. He tended to lose his temper over things like people mistreating animals or being careless. But she had never seen him like this. So utterly thunderous. And she had *certainly* never seen it directed at her. Even Ruby shrank back as he strode across towards her.

'Do you have any idea what could have happened?' he glowered. 'What the hell were you thinking?'

'I wasn't thinking,' she said, wishing her voice wasn't cracking.

'You don't need to tell me that,' he snapped. 'I'm well aware you weren't thinking. Gordon was out there looking for you. *Gordon!* He's in his sixties! Do you realise what could've happened? Do you?'

She sat up in bed, her heart pounding. 'Of course I realise what could've happened!'

'Of all the bloody irresponsible things—'

'I made a mistake! I know that! You think I don't know that?'

She was inches away from him. Close enough to feel the rage

radiating from his body. To see the way his breaths were heaving with fury. But she was furious too. All she'd wanted was for him to pull her into him. To hold her against his chest, and instead, he was yelling at her. Not that she didn't deserve it. No, she deserved every harsh word that came her way.

'Well, you were right about one thing at least,' he huffed.

'I was?' Her heart spiked, though the fire in her eyes remained.

'It was a good job you called things quits between us. There's no way you're cut out for life up here if you think you can just wander off like that.'

Tears filled her eyes and throat as she struggled to stifle her sob. She wasn't going to let him see just how much those words stung.

'Of all the selfish things you could have —'

'That's enough.'

The voice came from the doorway, and to Bex's surprise, Kieron was standing there and his face was almost as thunderous as Duncan's.

'This is a private conversation,' Duncan snapped back, the muscles in his jaw grinding together.

'It's hardly private when you're yelling at the top of your voice in my home,' Kieron said sharply. 'You've made your point. You can go.'

A bitter chuckle rose from Duncan's throat. 'Oh, I'm not even started. She could've died!'

'She knows that. But she didn't.' Kieron took another three steps into the room, only stopping when he was perfectly squared up to Duncan. The Scotsman had at least four inches of height on Kieron, but he matched him pound for pound in pure intimidation. 'Rebecca knows exactly what happened here. But thankfully, she's okay. You, however, will not be. Not if you raise your voice to her like that again. Now, get out of here, before I have to make you.'

Bex was holding her breath. Duncan wasn't a man who would look for fights. Ever. He was the type of person who broke them up. But she had never seen him look like this before. Like every rational sense had been overcome by something completely primal.

His glower shifted between Bex and Kieron, then back to Bex. Her breath continued to quiver in her lungs as she was certain he was about to tell her again what a complete idiot she was, or perhaps how foolish he had ever been to love her. But instead, he let out a low, growl-like sound before turning sharply.

As she finally released her breath, his footsteps thundered down the hallway before fading into the distance.

'I'm so sorry,' Kieron said, dropping down onto the edge of the bed beside Ruby. His hand reached out, stroking the dog absent-mindedly behind her ears. 'I shouldn't have let him in. If I'd thought for one moment that he was going to speak to you like that, I would have thrown him out of the castle. And his lodge too for that matter.'

As the adrenaline caused by Duncan's anger ebbed from her body, Bex found her hands trembling.

'He was just worried,' she said. The last thing she needed was for him to lose the lodge over this too. 'He was worried and didn't know what to do.'

'The temper on some of these locals...' Kieron shook his head as he let out a scoff, but then his eyes met Bex's and his expression softened. 'Then again, I suspect I'd have been pretty furious too if I'd been stupid enough to let you go. Although, I'd have been gentlemanly enough not to take it out on you.'

It wasn't the comment itself that caught her off guard, but the warmth in his tone as he spoke. The way he looked at her had almost as much of a soothing effect as the dog beside her. And speaking of Ruby, for someone who didn't think animals should be pets, Kieron looked incredibly relaxed scratching behind her ears.

'Thank you,' Bex said softly. 'For everything. I'm so sorry for making a mess of things. And for not telling you about Duncan. It just seemed easier if you didn't know. Less complicated.'

Kieron nodded as he stood up. 'You've nothing to apologise for. You're okay. We're all okay.'

She sat up a little, wishing that Kieron had remained sitting with her for just a little longer at least. 'I really appreciate it.'

His smile glinted, and with it, that familiar light shone in his irises. 'You are most welcome. Now, I need to fetch you that drink. Just lie down and relax, okay?'

As Bex shuffled slightly, Kieron leaned forward and over the bed. Her pulse soared. Was he leaning in to kiss her? Her mind raced as her eyes fixed on his. The moment was seemingly happening in slow motion. He was still moving towards her. His lips getting closer and closer. Was that what she wanted? She didn't know, but would it really be that bad to find out?

The way Duncan had spoken to her, it was clear there was no redemption left in that relationship. Ever. And Kieron... Kieron had saved her life. Kieron had made it clear that he liked her. Respected her. Bended his rules and allowed dogs on the bed for her.

Without giving herself the chance to second-guess her actions, she leaned forward and pressed her lips to his. A taste of winter and whisky flooded her as he responded just as she'd hoped. His mouth parted slightly as he pressed towards her but then, suddenly, without warning, he pulled back and cleared his throat.

'I... I was going to adjust your pillow,' he said, his cheeks brightening with a pink hue.

Never had Bex wanted a bed to swallow her whole quite as much as she did in that moment.

'Oh God, I'm so sorry,' she stammered, feeling heat flood through her body. It should have been welcome, given the freezing state of her bones, but right now it wasn't. 'I didn't mean... I wasn't... I shouldn't have. Crap.'

Kieron smiled gently.

'I'm not saying that I minded, but how about you try that again when you haven't just been through a massive trauma?'

Bex shook her head, horrified by what she had just done. 'I'm so sorry—' she started again, only for him to cut her off.

'Don't you dare apologise,' he said. 'I just think our first kiss shouldn't be when you're in bed wearing my pyjamas.'

He stood and smiled. 'I'll send Gordon up with a hot chocolate. Try to get some rest, all right?'

As the door closed behind him, Bex sank back into her pillow and covered her face with her hands.

How had she been so stupid? That was ridiculous. There was no chance she was going to get any sleep now.

Well. That was certainly one way to make an impression.

33

Bex had no concept of time. Gordon came up a little while after Kieron had left, with a hot chocolate and some shortbread biscuits and told her to drink as much as she could. She tried taking a couple of mouthfuls, but what she really needed was sleep.

'I'm sorry, Gordon,' she said as she forced another mouthful of sugar into her body. 'I'm sorry that you had to go out there looking for me. It was stupid and selfish.'

'Hush, lass,' he said, shaking his head. 'You're all good. And ye' know I love a reason to get out a' that study.'

She tried to laugh, grateful that he was trying to make light of things, but she struggled. It turned out being stranded in the snow was a great way to zap the energy from your body.

'Do you think you could bring me my bag up from the office? My phone?' she asked when she'd drunk as much as she could manage.

'Aye. Sure thing.'

She wasn't going to ring anyone. There was no point. It was not as if her friends and family back in England could do anything. Ringing them would just cause them to panic, which was unnecessary now that she was safe and warm. She just needed it there in case someone tried to get hold of her.

As it happened, though, she was already fast asleep when Gordon came back with her bag, and it was only when she opened her eyes, several hours later, to see the bedside lamp still on, that she realised the whole day had gone.

'Ruby?' she said as she glanced down at her feet and saw the bed was empty, though as she sat up, she discovered that not only was Ruby still in the room, with her favourite well-chewed pheasant toy between her legs, but that she had company too.

'Duncan told us what happened,' Lorna said, rushing over, closely followed by Eilidh. The pair scooched across the mattress so that they were sitting either side of Bex while Ruby, now aware that Bex was up and could once again give her attention, jumped back into her normal position at the foot of the bed.

'I am such an idiot,' Bex muttered.

'You won't hear any of us disagree with that,' Lorna replied, though Eilidh shot her friend a glare.

'It's not the first time it's happened around here,' Eilidh said, a little more gently. 'Although, yes, we did think a little better of you. How are you doing?'

Bex scoffed. It wasn't an easy question. Completely embarrassed. Ashamed. Humiliated. Those were the words that sprang to mind, though she suspected her friends were asking about the more physical side of things.

'Honestly? I'm feeling pretty lucky,' she said eventually. 'I'm knackered. It feels like my bones have been replaced with rusted steel, and my throat hurts like hell too, but I'm not sure if that's from the cold or from all the screaming I was doing.'

'Well, we're just so blooming relieved that you're okay,' Lorna said. Only then did Bex notice the red rims of her eyes. As if she'd been crying.

'Yeah, that makes both of us.'

Lorna pressed her lips together, hesitating before speaking again. 'Kieron said Duncan was pretty harsh with you. He was fair boilin'.'

'Well, that's one way of putting it,' Bex said, loving the Scottish turn of phrase. 'He had a few choice words. I think it's fair to say there's no love lost there any more.'

'You don't believe that,' Lorna said sharply. 'He was just worried. Because he loves you. You get that, right?'

Bex wanted to believe her, but then Lorna had not heard what Duncan had said. It wasn't just how he'd spoken, but the words he'd chosen too. Saying how it was a good job they'd called it quits. She wanted to tell her friends as much, but the words got trapped in her throat.

Instead, she let out a sigh before pulling in a slightly sharper breath and trying to sound proactive. 'Kieron said he's happy for me to stay here,' she said, directing her words at Lorna. 'But if I'm honest, I'd rather we went home to yours. If that's okay with you?'

'Of course it's ok—' Lorna cut herself off before she could finish the last syllable of the word. 'When you say we...?'

Bex glanced at the dog lying at her feet. Eilidh had currently taken on the role of chief scratcher and was busy working away at a spot behind Ruby's ear. As she looked back at Lorna, Bex offered her the best puppy dog eyes she could manage.

'She saved my life,' she said. 'And she's been ill herself.'

With a long sigh, Lorna looked at the dog before rolling her eyes. 'Well, I guess I can't say no to that, can I?'

* * *

Bex's clothes had been drying by the fire, but as she went to undo the buttons on the pyjamas, she found her fingers struggling and decided to just slip her coat over the top of them. After all, she needed to give them a wash before returning them to Kieron. And they were incredibly comfortable.

Eilidh held her by the arm as they headed down the staircase. There, waiting at the bottom, was Kieron.

Bex slipped her arm out of Eilidh's as she walked over to him.

'Are you sure you don't want to stay?' he asked her.

'I am. Thank you, though. Thank you so much for everything. I can't apologise enough.'

'And I've already told you – you don't need to. It's fine.'

He reached out and took her hand, their fingers interlacing. 'Just to be clear, I do not want to see you at work tomorrow. You hear me? I want you to rest up, properly. Because if you can't dance with me on Burns Night, well, then you're going to have something to really apologise for.'

She let out a slight laugh before leaning forward and kissing him on the cheek.

'See you soon, Kieron.'

'I certainly hope so,' he replied.

Back at Lorna's, Ruby immediately claimed a spot on the sofa. Given how it was also Bex's bed, and substantially smaller than the one at the castle, she was fairly sure it was going to be a tight squeeze when she wanted to go to bed, but she didn't care. She would sleep on the floor if it meant keeping Ruby beside her.

'Just so you know, if that ugly duck thing ends up in my bed, I will put it straight in the bin,' Lorna said, though whether the comment was directed at Ruby or herself, Bex couldn't tell.

'It's a pheasant,' Bex responded. 'And don't worry, it won't. You're going to be on your best behaviour, right, Rubes?' The dog wagged her tail as she reached up and licked Bex's cheek in response.

'And no licking me either,' Lorna added. 'I'm not a licking person.'

Eilidh had driven them home – her truck better in the snow than Lorna's little car – but had promised to go over to Niall's to fill him in on everything that had happened.

'So, I hear it was a race to rescue you,' Lorna said as she handed Bex another hot chocolate, this time spiked with Irish cream. It seemed to be the current remedy for everything, and while Bex wasn't sure she could stomach another one, she held on to it anyway, out of politeness.

'I know, and I'm so grateful they got me in time. So grateful you showed them where I was, right, girl?'

'That's not exactly what I meant,' Lorna replied. 'I mean, I'm grateful too, but I meant *Kieron versus Duncan*. Seems like the new laird is quite keen on you.'

Bex didn't think there was any point in denying it. 'He asked me if I'd come to Burns Night as his date,' she said.

'What did you say?'

'That I'd think about it. And he was fine with that.' Bex paused, wondering how much she should share with Lorna, but now she had started talking, it seemed silly to stop. 'I didn't mention this to you earlier, but I actually met him before I got here. He was at the airport with me. I sort of swiped his ankles with my suitcase, and we had a bit of a moment there. And another one before we boarded.' She remembered the napkin he had given her. Folded over, with his number written in the centre.

'Why didn't you say anything?' Lorna replied, her eyes widening in surprise. Bex shrugged.

'I wasn't sure what to say. It's not like anything happened – or would happen. Not with... well...'

'With Duncan,' Lorna finished for her.

'I get that he was angry earlier,' Bex said, breathless. 'But you should've heard him, Lorna. It was like he despised me.'

Lorna coughed. 'Duncan could never despise you. Believe me, he adores you.'

'You didn't see him. Trust me, I've never seen anyone that angry. I get that I deserved it, but he was so horrid.'

'And Kieron?' Lorna prompted.

Bex couldn't quite put it into words. Kieron had been gentle with her, understanding, non-judgemental – basically everything Duncan hadn't been, even though she had needed him the most in that moment. If Duncan had wrapped his arms around her, told her he loved her and needed her, she would've wilted into him, letting all the difficulties fall away. But he hadn't. Kieron had been the one who was there.

An urge flooded through Bex. The urge to tell Lorna what had happened.

'I kissed him,' she blurted out.

'What? When?'

'When we were in the bedroom... I don't know what I was thinking. Well, I'd thought he was going in to kiss me and he wasn't, but I kissed him anyway.'

Lorna had moved past the wide-eyes stage and was now staring at Bex, her jaw near unhinged.

'So what's going to happen now?' she asked.

Bex shrugged. She wasn't trying to be coy. She just really didn't have a clue.

'I don't know. I know I like him. I do. But he's not, not...'

'Not Duncan?' Lorna finished for her.

Bex nodded. 'Yeah. But then Duncan made it very clear that there's no chance of him and me rekindling things. Even if I wanted to.'

As Bex waited for a reply, Lorna narrowed her eyes as she tilted her head to the side. 'But I thought you didn't want to rekindle things? That's what you've been saying to everyone since you got here. That it wouldn't work. That it was better in the long run that—'

'Yes, I get it,' Bex cut in. The last thing she needed was to hear every word she had said about why she and Duncan shouldn't be together. But then, how did she explain her change of heart? Because he was the person she had thought about when she'd thought she was going to die. That having him yelling at her was better than not having him in her life at all. That just sounded ridiculous.

And if one of her friends had ever come to her and said that, she'd know exactly what she'd have told them. It was the trauma. They weren't thinking straight. They needed some time to recover and get their thoughts together.

So that was what she was going to let herself do.

'What's he like?' she said instead.

'Who? Kieron?'

'Yeah.'

Lorna drew in a long breath. 'I don't know. I mean, no one seems to have much to say about him. Except Duncan. He hates the guy, in case you didn't pick up on that.'

'I had noticed,' Bex replied. 'Did something happen between the pair of them?'

'I don't think so,' Lorna said as she shook her head and crinkled her nose. 'I think Kieron was a bit of an arse when they were kids. Referring to him as the help and stuff. And Duncan's always thought Kieron should do more for the community, you know. As the heir and everything. But that's because Duncan's happy to give his whole life to the castle and village, and he can't understand when someone else won't do the same. Especially not when they're going to inherit it one day.'

Bex pondered the words. Duncan did give his all to this place, which was the reason she couldn't be with him. Not because she'd come second. No, she was okay with that. It was giving everything else up that she couldn't do. A job. A corner office. London life. None of which she'd thought of as she sat there shivering in the cold.

'Clearly he's gorgeous.' Lorna continued to talk about Kieron in a slightly more upbeat manner. 'And he throws incredible parties. Oh my God, if you did get together with him, imagine the wedding at the castle. How amazing would that be? Not that I'm pushing you and Kieron, obviously. I have to be team Duncan all the way. You understand that. But a castle wedding would be phenomenal.'

Bex chuckled. 'Of course I understand.'

Her laughter faded almost as quickly as it had started.

'So only five days until Burns Night,' Lorna said. 'I guess you've got until then to decide whether you're going to be his date.'

34

Lorna went to bed a little after Bex had told her about the kiss with Kieron, and it was only when she then looked at her phone that she saw it was after ten. Ten in the evening, and she hadn't done a single hour's work. Part of her wondered if she should ring Nigel and tell him that she had been sick – it was the closest she was going to come to telling him what had happened – but she was near enough a junior director now. She could be trusted to take days off only when she needed it. Besides, it wasn't like it affected her work in London. That had already all been delegated. So instead, with Ruby having moved over to the armchair, she closed her eyes, ready to start again in the morning.

Only that didn't quite go to plan.

'Bex? Bex, I think you ought to wake up now.' Lorna's voice was accompanied by a slight shake on Bex's shoulder. 'I know you want to sleep, but I think you really need to eat something.'

Bex blinked a couple of times, only to find that her head was pounding. The dull throb was affecting every part of her skull from her forehead to the top of her neck. She lifted her hand, rubbing her temples, though her fingertips had barely made contact with her skin, when Lorna placed a hand on her back, pushing her up into a sitting position.

'Here, I think you need to drink this,' she said, handing Bex a large glass. 'I read online that in cases of near hyperthermia, you can suffer from dehydration. So drink up.'

Dehydration? That would explain the pounding head, Bex thought. But near hyperthermia? It still terrified her to think how close she had come to tragedy the day before. But it wasn't something she wanted to dwell on. After sitting fully, she took a sip, expecting to taste the crisp cleanness of water, when instead a salty tang caused her to cough and gag.

'What is that?' she asked, looking at the glass for the first time properly and noting that the liquid inside had a definite greenish hue.

'Rehydration salts,' Lorna answered. 'It'll help, I promise. Dehydration, remember.'

With a slight sniff, Bex took another sip. It still didn't taste any better, but at least she was prepared. She swallowed a couple of mouthfuls, still aware of the pounding in her skull, then reached to put the glass on the coffee table in front of her, only to let out a low groan.

'Oh my God, everything hurts,' she said, discovering that the aching throbs weren't restricted to her head. It was like she was suffering from a killer hangover, without any of the fun from the drinking beforehand.

'It's going to take you a while to recover,' Lorna said, taking the glass from her and placing it down. 'I did a bit of googling. The headache and muscle aches are normal. As is the excessive sleeping.'

'Excessive sleeping?' Bex asked, reaching for her phone, only to stop as her body groaned in protest.

'Aye, it's just gone two, and you hadn't even fluttered your eyelids open.'

'What? Two o'clock in the afternoon?' Bex stiffened, preparing to leap from the bed. Only her body seized with pain as she twisted. 'Oh my God,' she said, clutching her head.

'You might want to lie back down.' Lorna spoke with the authority of someone who had been using the internet and now assumed they were qualified to distribute medical advice. That was what Bex assumed, at least, until her friend carried on talking. 'When the doctor saw you he said you'd probably need rest, but that I should try to wake you up and get you to drink something.'

'I saw a doctor? When did that happen?' How out of it had she been? Surely she would have remembered seeing a doctor.

'Yesterday,' Lorna explained. 'When they got you back to the castle. He said to ring him today if you were struggling to think properly, but I figured I had to wake you up to know that.'

Bex certainly felt like she was struggling to think properly. How the heck could she have slept that long? It was Friday. She was meant to be at work. Kieron and Gordon had both said she could take as long as she needed before coming back to the castle, but she'd assumed that would mean having a bit of a lie in. Not missing an entire day.

'Finish up your electrolytes and you can have another hot chocolate before I make some food,' Lorna continued. 'We need to make sure you try to keep your energy up.'

Keeping her energy up sounded like a good idea, as even after nearly sixteen hours' sleep, Bex was desperate to close her eyes and sleep a little longer. But there was something in what Lorna had said that made her pause. After all, near hypothermia or not, there were only so many hot chocolates one person could handle in twenty-four hours.

'Food sounds like a good idea, but any chance I could just get a cup of tea instead?' Bex asked. 'With lots of sugar, obviously.'

As Lorna headed into the kitchen, Bex slowly manoeuvred herself and noticed the reddish-brown mass of fur curled up on the armchair.

'Oh crap!' she said.

'What is it?' Lorna bolted straight in from the kitchen. 'Is it your fingers? Is it tingling, or numbness? Can you remember what your date of birth is?'

'Yes, I mean no, I mean... My fingers are fine and yes, I know when I was born. It's just Ruby. She's been here all day. She needs a walk.'

Relief washed across Lorna's face, and Bex saw with a surge of guilt just how worried her friends had been about her.

'Oh, God, you had me scared. Don't worry about Ruby. Duncan came round and took care of her.'

'He did?'

Lorna nodded. 'Aye, he came over first thing. And then before midday. I think he was hoping for a chance to apologise, but I wouldn't let him in. You were fast asleep, and I thought the last thing you needed was him yelling at you again.'

A flash of warmth rippled through Bex. She knew how much Lorna adored her big brother, and how she would do pretty much anything he asked of her. It was a testament to their friendship that she hadn't let him in.

'Thank you. I really appreciate it.'

'No problem.' Lorna smiled, as if she knew what Bex was thinking. 'I'll fetch that tea.'

When Lorna returned, Bex took the drink. There was a definite throbbing behind her temples, and her fingers felt as though they were burning. How was it possible for them to feel so hot after being frozen stiff?

'So, only four days left till Burns Night. Are you ready?'

'By "ready", do you mean ready to decide if I want to accept Kieron's date? Then absolutely not. I've no idea what I'm doing with him, and I'm trying not to think about it,' Bex said truthfully. 'But if you mean ready to experience this big night that you Scots make the most of? Then possibly. Assuming I can get out of bed, that is.'

'You better.' Lorna grinned. 'I'll carry you there myself. Look, I've got to go. I've got a shift at the pub, but you take today and rest. Gordon's not expecting you. You could even take the week off if you wanted.'

'I'm not going to do that,' Bex said.

'I know, but I thought I'd give you the option. It might help keep you here a bit longer, after all.' As Lorna stood there, a sad smile flittered across her face. Was it because the memory of nearly losing Bex was still incredibly raw or because she knew that when this job was over, Bex would be going back to London? And as much as she wanted to say she'd come back and visit, they both knew it wouldn't happen. Not for a long time anyway. Not when things with Duncan were still so raw.

She opened her mouth to tell Lorna that, no matter what, it wasn't going to affect their friendship and if she had to fly up to Edinburgh or meet elsewhere for girly weekends to keep the friendship going, then that was what she'd do. But before she got a chance to get a word out, a shrill beeping cut through the cottage, searing through Bex's skull and sending Ruby leaping from the armchair.

'Shit!' Lorna yelled as the smell of smoke wafted in from the kitchen. 'That was your food.'

35

Bex couldn't help but wonder if Duncan would pop round in the afternoon as well, given that he'd already dropped in twice to try to speak to her, but as the evening rolled around and Lorna left her to work at the pub, she found herself on her own. Other than with Ruby.

'We're going to have to work out this whole London thing,' she said as she looked at the dog. 'I mean, technically I'm not supposed to have dogs in my apartment, but there are plenty of people who do. It's you I'm worried about, though. There aren't the open fields you've got here. And I'll have to work during the day. I'm not sure I'll be allowed to take you into the office. Not that you'd want to be in there, really. It's not nearly as comfy as the study.'

Although there would be room for a dog bed in her corner office, she considered, the thought didn't cause quite as much excitement as it had when she'd first learned about it. Maybe it was because of Ruby. She wanted to take the dog with her. One hundred per cent. But would it be fair, when she had a perfect life up here, with people who loved her just as much? The situation held far too many parallels to the other Scottish love in Bex's life, and she decided it wasn't worth thinking about at the moment, anyway. She didn't need to decide what to do until she left, and that wouldn't be for a few days yet.

Never could Bex remember a weekend when she had slept as much. She woke up near midday on both Saturday and Sunday, by which time Duncan had already taken Ruby for a long walk, then remained on the sofa watching films, either with Lorna, or on her own when Lorna was picking up shifts at the pub and café. When Daisy and Claire rang for a chat on Sunday morning, Bex tried to act normal and pretend like everything was fine, but the minute they saw her on the screen, they knew something had happened.

'I just spent too long out in the cold,' she said as casually as possible. 'I forgot what the winters are like up here. But don't worry, I'm being well taken care of.'

'By Duncan?' Daisy said with more than a little hint of hope in her voice.

'No,' Bex replied firmly. 'By Lorna. But Duncan has taken Ruby for walks for me.'

'You've got Ruby?' Claire said. 'How come? I thought you said she was living with Duncan now?'

Bex cursed herself for such a stupid slip up.

'She just made it clear that she wants to spend a bit more time with me,' Bex said, praying they bought it.

Thankfully, the conversation swiftly moved on to Claire's daughter Amelia, who was going through her first teenage heartbreak, and Bex listened in, offering only the occasional contribution. After all, it wasn't like she could give anyone advice on how to move on after love. Real love, anyway. Not the infatuation-based feelings that her previous relationships had tried to mask as the real deal.

That night, she took a long hot bath, then set several alarms for the morning, determined she wasn't going to miss any more work. Although while she got out of bed without any issue, convincing Lorna she was okay to go to work was another matter.

'No one's going to think anything of you if you spend another day in bed.' Her friend's arms were folded firmly across her chest as she spoke. 'Whatever this cloak and dagger thing you and Gordon are doing, you can have a couple of days off. I mean, if you tell me what it is you're trying to do, maybe I could help?' Her eyebrow raised playfully.

'Nice try,' Bex said. 'And it's not cloak and dagger. It's just legal things, that's all.' Lorna didn't look convinced, but Bex continued anyway. 'Honestly, I'll be fine. I need to get out.'

Lorna huffed. 'Fine. I'll give you a lift in, but I'm going to speak to Gordon myself and tell him that if you look even a wee peely-wally he's to bring you home.'

'Peely-wally' wasn't a term Bex had ever heard her friend use before, but she stored it away for future reference. Another part of the condition was that Bex was not to take Ruby for a walk, either. Instead, Lorna dropped the dog off at Duncan's and told her he was going to bring her back to her cottage in the evening. Bex tried her hardest to hide her annoyance at her ex. He had gone from trying to speak to her to no longer being able to speak to her. Talk about mixed signals.

As much as she hoped Gordon had miraculously found the missing piece of their jigsaw on the Friday, Bex thoroughly doubted he had and was still certain that talking to Moira was their best bet. She intended to say as much to him. Only first she had to get to him. And Lorna wasn't the only problem. The situation at the castle wasn't quite as she'd expected.

'Is this all for Burns Night?' she asked herself when she'd squeezed her way through countless people outside and in the hallway. There were caterers with large serving carts and metal trays, and a group of four people carrying two of the biggest speakers she had ever seen. Even when she found Gordon in the study, it was near impossible to hold an actual conversation, what with people setting up coat racks and a bar directly next door. It didn't help that no one really knew where they were supposed to be going, and every two minutes the door opened with another person asking how they got to the dining hall, or the ballroom or the kitchen.

As much as she wished it wasn't the case, every time the door cracked open, a surge of adrenaline hit as she both feared and hoped that perhaps it was Kieron or Duncan wanting to talk. Yet there had been no sign of Duncan and the only time she'd seen Kieron he had been so absorbed in what he was doing, he hadn't even noticed her.

Half of her was expecting Duncan to come in grovelling with apologies, but there had been no sign of him.

With the noise level almost unbearable, she and Gordon moved to the library, where she discovered drawers beneath the lower levels of the bookcases containing legal documents and one or two ledgers that should have been included in her initial accounting. Thankfully, it wasn't too difficult to work them into her updated reports.

'Do we have a plan for if we don't find this "rightful heir"?' she asked as she moved to slip the ledgers into her bag, finding them surprisingly heavy. She wanted it to be because of the size, but she was well aware that her recovery hadn't been quite so complete as she'd made out to Lorna or Gordon.

Gordon pursed his lips as he took off his glasses. 'Well, if the heir cannae be found, it'll fall tae Kieron. At least until someone comes forward to contest it. But that'll get even messier then. And I know we'll have to broach the subject with him at some point. He's no' gonna stop asking me about the will, and there are only so many times I can tell him it's just taking time.'

'Surely he knows that estates this size come with a lot of red tape.'

'Och, he knows. But he also knows we're keeping things from him. Smart lad, that one. Seems tae think a lot of you too, if the other day is anything to go on. Same as Duncan. 'Nother good lad he is too.'

His gaze narrowed on Bex, but as much as she liked Gordon, this was not something she wanted to discuss with him.

'Are you coming to Burns Night?' she said, less than subtly trying to shift the conversation away from the men in her life. Though her plan was foiled by a rap on the door, which then immediately opened. Kieron stood in the doorway, looking directly at Bex.

'Speak o' the devil,' Gordon muttered, though Kieron didn't seem to hear.

'Rebecca, I thought I heard your voice,' he said, striding over to her. 'I didn't expect to see you in. How are you doing? Are you sure you don't need to rest some more? I'm sure Gordon could manage without you for a little while.' A thin line furrowed between his brows; a look of genuine concern on his face.

'I'm fine, honestly,' Bex said, ignoring how difficult she had found it to lift the ledgers only a moment before. 'I think it's better to keep me busy, you know. I'm the kind of person who needs to keep moving.'

'You are remarkable,' he said, shaking his head, as if he was in absolute awe of her.

'I don't feel remarkable right now,' Bex replied. 'My chest feels like I've swallowed a porcupine. Not to mention the embarrass- ment. I'm pretty sure the entire village knows what happened.'

'Oh, I'm sure they do.' He smirked. 'Village life. Hence you and I are the eternal city dwellers at heart.'

His eyes locked on her, though she could have sworn they shifted down to her lips, for only a heartbeat. As if recalling their kiss – and perhaps hoping to recreate the moment again. Was that something Bex wanted to do? She really wasn't sure at all, but when Gordon cleared his throat behind her, she realised that even if she had wanted to, it was definitely not the right time to do so.

'I should leave you to get to work,' Kieron said, his smirk rising to something more coy as he remained looking at her. 'I'll see you tomorrow night, though. For the party.'

'You will,' Bex said. 'I'm looking forward to it.'

'You and me both,' he said, before offering one more smile, then turned and strode out of the room.

As Kieron closed the door behind him, Bex turned back to find Gordon, wearing a smirk on his face, though this one was very different to Kieron's.

'Told you he's soft on you,' he said, quirking an eyebrow.

'Oh, do be quiet,' Bex snapped, picking up the nearest notebook to her and opening it on a random page. 'We've got work to do.'

36

Although the twenty-fifth of January wasn't technically a holiday, it certainly felt like one in the village.

Once again, Lorna had insisted on driving Bex down to the castle, and she wasn't going to complain. The previous day had left her more exhausted than she would have imagined – especially considering she'd spent most of the day sitting down. But she'd woken up that morning with a sense of energy, which was good, because she really needed to give Ruby a walk. And not least because she didn't want Duncan thinking she needed help taking care of her.

She hadn't broached the fact that she was planning on taking Ruby back to London to anyone yet – other than Ruby herself – but she knew that the only person who could potentially have a problem with it was Duncan. After all, he'd been with the dog since she was a pup and she was also one of his last ties to Fergus. Then again, there was no telling whether the future laird – whether that was indeed Kieron or this elusive rightful heir – would even let Duncan keep his role on the estate. They would be a fool if they didn't, but people did strange things.

As much as she tried not to speculate who this mystery person might be – after all, she doubted she'd even know them – it was hard not to wonder a little bit. Given Fergus's age, any child he'd had would have easily been as old as her parents. So was that the age of person they were looking for? Or perhaps, rather than a son or daughter, they were looking for a grandchild. That would make them more her age, which meant if they were local, then she might even know them.

'Get out the way, you daft eejit!' Lorna yelled out of her car window as she hammered her fist on the horn.

The narrow road that bisected the village was buzzing with Land Rovers and 4x4s going back and forth. She didn't know if the vehicles belonged to guests or just people bringing things to the castle, but either way, there was a definite party vibe in the air.

'Is it always like this?' Bex asked as they crawled forward. There was no doubt that if they were going at this pace, it would be far quicker for her to walk to the castle, but she wasn't going to say as much to Lorna. As it was, she was in no great rush to get to the castle. She wasn't too sure what they were going to do there. Though when she arrived and found Gordon in the library, wrestling with a bundle of keys, she soon found out.

'I thought we should just lock anything that could point to what we're doing away in the cupboards,' he told Bex. 'People tend to get drunk and wander at these events, and Kieron wouldnae take too kindly to me suggesting we lock entire rooms.'

'Do you really think that's necessary?' Bex said, looking at the haphazard piles of paper around them. 'I mean, we've not been able to find any answers from looking at all this. I can't imagine that anyone who doesn't know why we're here would have a clue what we're looking for.'

Gordon's chin bobbed in a nod as he scratched the bridge of his nose.

'You're probably right, but I'd feel better if we at least had everything out of sight.'

'Fair enough,' Bex said. 'Well, I'll head to the study, make sure everything's okay there, if you're all right.'

'I'm grand,' Gordon said. 'And dinnae fuss about working all day today. You get home whenever you need. Reckon you've got a fair bit to get ready the nicht.'

That was one way of putting it. Lorna had arranged an entire afternoon of appointments, from hair and nails to a dress fitting with Eilidh, and final preparations to get ready for the event. But given how Bex was still feeling guilty for the previous week's events, she was keen to make the most of the few hours she was there.

The study felt strangely empty, especially without even Ruby there, sitting in her armchair. Bex got to work. She really did think that Gordon was overreacting. There was no chance that people would see these stacks of paperwork and assume that Fergus's will mentioned something about another heir. But her role was to help Gordon, and that was what she was going to do.

She moved to the cupboard to store away a couple of folders when a small leather notebook dropped out. It was the one she had seen several times before; the one with the names of hospitals in it. An entire notebook containing nothing but a list of hospital names, all of which had been neatly crossed through.

It was a lovely notebook. Worn tan leather with thick lined paper inside. The type of quality Bex wasn't sure you could even get any more, certainly not without paying through the nose for it. If it had been hers, she would've ripped out or replaced that first page and started fresh. But it wasn't hers. It was Fergus's, or

Kieron's, or whoever everything of the old laird's now belonged to.

Besides, she could never damage anything that had belonged to the old laird. Even a seemingly meaningless notebook. She lifted it up, slipped it back onto the pile in the cupboard and shut the door.

It was just after eleven when Gordon told her she should head back. It hardly seemed fair, given that she'd only done a few hours' work, but he insisted.

'Trust me, it's going to get so loud in here soon you won't be able to do anything. Give me a minute, and I'll give you a lift back to the village.'

Bex hesitated. The sky outside was clear and blue. Yes, it was cold, but there wasn't a hint of cloud, let alone a threat of snow. This wasn't like the walk she'd taken before, across the fields where it was easy to get lost. She was going to walk straight back to the village, along paths she had trodden hundreds of times.

'If you don't mind,' Bex said, 'I really feel like I could do with the exercise. I've barely had a chance to stretch my legs.'

Gordon's cheeks puffed out slightly as he considered how to respond. Bex wouldn't put up a fight if he insisted on giving her a lift – that would hardly be reasonable – but with Lorna mollycoddling her so much lately, she really needed a bit of space.

'Fine, but I need you to send me a message,' Gordon said eventually, 'the minute you're back in the village.'

'Yes, Dad,' Bex replied, but she couldn't help but grin. Gordon really did have a paternal air about him and it caused a warmth to fill her, especially given how far away she was from her own. That had been another reason Bex had never been able to see herself settling here. Being away from her family. Her friends. People she knew. Yet it never ceased to amaze her how many people there were in this little village that genuinely cared about her. And now it felt like she could add Gordon to that list too. She turned to leave before hesitating and looking back at the old man.

'I guess I'll see you tonight, won't I? You are coming?'

He crinkled his nose and let out a slight huff.

'We'll see,' he said. 'And don't forget about that text all right?'

The walk back was everything she needed. Fresh air to fill her lungs. Wide open space. It was ridiculous to think that a place this beautiful, this calm and serene, had been so deadly only a few days before. But it wasn't a lesson she was going to forget anytime soon. If ever.

When she reached the cottage, Bex let herself in, thinking how strange it would be to go back to her own apartment, to sleep in her own bed. Lorna's sofa bed, as temporary as it was, was incredibly comfortable, but Bex had been there for over a week now. She really needed to consider booking a B&B to stop imposing on Lorna, and since the business would cover the cost, it seemed like a fair solution. Not that Lorna would take too kindly to it. Bex was well aware of how much she enjoyed having a housemate. And given the night they were about to have, today didn't feel like the right time to bring it up.

'Hey, girl,' Bex said as Ruby bounded up to her. 'You're back earlier than I thought you'd be. Did Lorna pick you up from Duncan's after your walk? Where is she? Is she here? Lorna, I'm back,' Bex called out as she stopped stroking Ruby long enough to slip off her shoes and hang up her coat. 'I'm ready to learn what all the fuss for tonight is about.' She walked into the living room, with her phone in her hand as she wrote her message to Gordon, saying she was back. As she typed away, her peripheral vision caught sight of someone sitting on the sofa. Lorna, she assumed. Only when she pressed send on the message and lifted her head up, it wasn't Lorna she found herself looking at at all.

It was Duncan.

'Can we talk?' he asked.

37

Ruby was standing between the pair of them, as if she wasn't sure who she was supposed to go to, though the back-and-forth motion of her head only accentuated the silence between them.

'I'm guessing you let yourself in with a spare key.' Bex didn't phrase it as a question. No matter how hard it had been for Lorna, she had tried to remain neutral when it came to the Duncan-Bex situation – unlike some other people – and there was no way that she would have let Duncan ambush Bex like this.

Rather than replying, Duncan stood up and pulled at the long strands of his beard, his gaze on the floor.

'I owe you an apology,' he said quietly.

'You think?' Bex's voice was stone cold. A surprise even to herself.

He lifted his head. Every part of his face, from the desperation in his eyes to the way he parted his lips, was full of remorse. 'I'm sorry. I really am.' He moved as if he was going to take a step towards her, only to stop and shake his head. 'I just lost it. I was terrified, and I was furious, and I shouldn't have been. I know I shouldn't have. I'm sorry.'

She let out a slight scoff. 'The things you said, Duncan... they were horrible.'

'I know, and it's not an excuse, but you scared the life out of me, Bex. I've never felt like that. I didn't know it was possible to feel that way.'

As much as she didn't want to, Bex knew the feeling he was talking about. It sounded remarkably like the fear that had flooded her when she'd been out in the cold; the strength seeping from her body as she thought she was never going to get another chance to speak to him. That had terrified her too. She opened her mouth to respond to him, but he continued, his voice trembling.

'I love you, Bex.' His voice was barely a whisper. 'I love you like I've never loved anyone else in my life. And when I thought I could've lost you, I couldn't think rationally. I couldn't... I couldn't... I'm sorry, for what I said. I was just scared of losing you. Losing you forever this time.'

His words brought tears to her eyes. Of course she knew he still loved her. Whatever flirting or other behaviours he indulged in with other women, she'd always known he loved her. That hadn't been why they had broken up.

'Lack of love was never our issue,' Bex said.

'No, it wasn't. I was.'

Bex's face crumpled in confusion. They had never assigned blame to their breakup, because no one had been at fault. Not really. Their futures just didn't align. That was all there was to it.

'Duncan,' she said softly. 'You and I—'

'No, listen, please,' he interrupted. 'I've thought about this.' He scoffed and let out a bitter laugh. 'I've pretty much thought o' nothing else since you came back to the village, and I need to get my words out, okay?'

She nodded, seeing how difficult this was for him. With a

deep breath in, he shuffled slightly, as if he was going to sit back down, but he didn't. Instead, he just moved a little further away from her. As if being close to her stopped him from being able to think.

'When you and I got together, I thought I was over Katty.'

'Katty?' The name surprised her. Katty was Duncan's ex-fiancée, who had cheated on him with his best friend. The pair had moved out of the village and had a baby and though she knew the loss of friendship had been hard on Duncan, he had never spoken that much about either of them.

'I thought I was over her when I got with you,' Duncan continued. 'And I was, in so many ways. I didn't want to be with her. I wanted to be with you. But I wasn't over what she did to me. I see that now. The hurt, the trust, it was all shattered. I was afraid, and I took those fears out on you. When you moved back to London, I told myself that I was doing everything I could to make the relationship work, but deep down, I know I didn't believe it. I didn't even try to make myself. I let the distance grow between us. Subconsciously or not I let myself believe it would be impossible for us to work. And then I let you believe it too.'

'And you're just realising this now?' Bex asked. Her voice sounded distant, harsh, but it was still kinder than the way he had spoken to her days ago.

'No, not just now. I think I always knew it on some level. What I've realised now is that I need to change who I am. I want to be with you. I *need* to be with you. You're it for me. And seeing you hurt. Seeing Kieron sitting there at your bedside...'

He let out a sound that was close to a growl. Something tightened in Bex's chest.

'Do you want to be with me, Duncan? Or do you want to be with me because Kieron wants to be with me? Because you didn't have a reaction like this when you saw me at the pub. When you were there with a pair of hot young women with their arms draped all over you.'

Duncan's jaw tightened.

'I realised it because I almost lost you,' he hissed. 'And you can't seriously think anything'll happen between you and Kieron.'

'Why?' Bex said, not sure why she was suddenly feeling so heated. Was it because she wanted to hit him, or kiss him? She couldn't tell. 'You're saying nothing could happen between us because he's a future laird and I'm just, me?'

'That's not what I meant at all.' Duncan lifted his hands in the air. 'You know that. I meant because he's not right for you. Besides, you barely know the guy.'

'From what I've heard, neither do you, and yet you still seem to think you know he's not right for me.'

'Yes,' Duncan said, taking another step towards her. He was close enough to take hold of her now. To kiss her. If that was what she wanted. Her body trembled, as it always did when he got too close. Like she couldn't control herself. 'Yes, I do,' he said again. 'I know he's not right because we're perfect together. You know that. I know you do. There's no one else for me, Barker. Not in this life, not in any that might be waiting for me afterwards. And I think it's the same for you too.'

He lifted his hand, brushing his fingers against her cheek. A small gasp left Bex's lips as warmth flooded her body. It was the opposite of the bone-chilling cold she'd felt during the storm. This warmth spread to her very core. It was all she wanted. It was everything she needed. Her chin tilted up towards him, and she was certain he was going to kiss her. And then what? Did it even matter for now?

Her heart hammered in her chest as she felt her eyes flutter closed, only for a voice to call in from the doorway.

'Bex, are you ready?' Lorna called. 'Sorry I'm late. We need to go get our hair done now or we'll miss our appointment.'

By the time Lorna stepped into the room, both Duncan and Bex had jumped so far apart they were practically on opposite sides of the room. Bex's pulse continued to drum behind her ears while her throat had turned so dry she wasn't even sure she could swallow.

'Duncan?' Lorna's voice lifted in surprise. 'What's going on? Is everything okay?'

Was it? Bex didn't have an answer, yet Duncan was looking at her like all this would fall on her. But this was hardly something she could make a decision on now. Her head was a blur.

'Everything's good,' she said, casting Lorna a quick smile. 'Duncan just brought Ruby back, that was all. He was about to leave, right?'

'Right,' Duncan replied after a beat, his expression unreadable as he walked forward and kissed Bex gently on the cheek. It was a parting kiss. The standard thing that friends would do when they said goodbye to one another, and yet she felt the rush of blood through her body as he turned and walked out the door. If nothing else, this trip had made one thing perfectly clear. She and Duncan would never just be friends.

38

'To Bex's first Burns Night!' Lorna said, lifting her glass into the centre of the group.

'Bex's first Burns Night.'

'Bex's first Burns Night!'

'My first Burns Night!'

The four of them clinked their glasses together before taking a sip of the bubbles.

The evening had rolled around fast and with it the knowledge that she was going to head to the castle and may or may not see Duncan again.

All afternoon, as Bex had sat in the hairdresser's chair, and then as one of Lorna's friends – who was studying at make-up college – applied her lip liner, and even as she'd had Eilidh perfectly fix the purple tartan over her shoulder, Bex's mind had been trapped back in that moment with Duncan. What would've happened if Lorna hadn't arrived home when she did? she wondered, although it wasn't a question that required much thought. She would've kissed him, for certain. That was what she'd wanted to do. But it still didn't change that seed of doubt at the bottom of her stomach.

Duncan said he would change to be with her. That he would get past his fears. And she didn't doubt that he would try. But that couldn't change the fact that their lives were in different parts of the country. Somehow she didn't think him getting over his fears would be enough for him to become a city dweller. So maybe the fact they hadn't kissed was a good thing. Maybe it would've just added more complications to the matter. Maybe he would simply always be the one that got away. Like Fergus, and the love of his life. No, of course it wasn't the same, but she couldn't help feel a sad parallel between the situations.

With the way her heart continued to throb, Bex could have lost hours reliving that near-kiss moment but now they were dressed, hair styled, make-up applied, and gathered at Lorna's cottage, ready for the evening. And the last thing she wanted to do was bring down her friends' moods with her own consternation. Besides, it was Burns Night. She wanted to enjoy it.

'So, how do you feel?' Eilidh asked.

'Nervous,' Bex replied truthfully.

'I meant about the outfit, not about tonight.'

'Oh.' Bex laughed as she took a drink before brushing a hand down the silky black fabric. 'It's perfect. Beyond perfect. I don't know how you're not showing your clothes at Paris fashion week already.'

Eilidh scoffed. 'It's not that special.'

'It is. It really is,' Bex insisted.

The design was simple, yet incredibly elegant – a black dress with a plunging cowl neckline and low back, while the tartan which was draped over her shoulders was fixed with a simple silver pin. It wasn't the V-neck she'd suggested; instead, it was infinitely more elegant.

'So, remind me. What happens when we get there?' she asked the group. 'I know there's dinner, but did I read something about poems too?'

'Poems and reading, then whisky, and then dancing. Lots and lots of dancing,' Niall replied. He was dressed in full tartan, complete with a kilt, and looked utterly dashing. From the way Eilidh couldn't keep her eyes off him, Bex suspected she felt the same. Maybe if there was enough whisky flowing, the two of them would finally own up to their feelings, but she doubted it. They'd had plenty of drunk opportunities to do so before, though Bex couldn't help but keep her fingers crossed. At least one of their group could do with their happily ever after.

'Right, well, our lift's gonna be here in five,' Eilidh said. 'We better drink up.'

'Roddy?' Bex asked, in reference to the lift.

'Obviously.' Lorna grinned back.

Roddy was the village dogsbody. He had originally worked for Fergus but often ended up doing whatever jobs needed to be done. He was the one who had driven Duncan and Bex back from their first official date and dropped them back at Duncan's lodge. He'd also dropped lunches in for Bex at the castle when Duncan hadn't been able to make it. He was a good bloke, and normally, she liked him, though when he picked them all up in their Burns Night's outfits, he immediately looked at Bex.

'Heard you were back,' he said. 'Make sure you gi'e me a text when you want picking up. Dinnae wan' you walkin' out in this weather. Again.'

'Why do people think I'm going to go out walking in a storm again?' Bex said as he got into the car. 'I have learned my mistake. Trust me. I'm never doing it again.'

'Fair enough,' Roddy muttered as he started the engine.

'Better hurry. We need to make sure you have time to take a seat before the haggis is piped in.'

'Piped in?' Bex asked.

'Do you really know nothing about this?'

'It'll make sense soon enough.'

After dropping them off, Roddy drove immediately back to the village. Apparently, he had another two drop-offs to do and had already done four before picking them up. By the sounds of things, it was going to be a good night for him, money-wise, anyway.

While Bex didn't immediately discover what the haggis's role was, the pipes became evident before they had even stepped inside the castle. The unmistakable tones of the bagpipes drifted through the air, causing a nervous excitement to flutter through her. There was so much to Scottish culture that she loved, and she didn't think this night was going to be any different.

When they headed past the drawing room and study, down the corridor, towards the dining hall, Bex was forced to do a double take. No wonder the workers had been so loud. The place was transformed. The wood-panelled ceiling was covered in sheer black drapes, interspersed with ivy garlands that sparkled with thousands of fairy lights while a long table had been set down the centre, with candles and tartan napkins with more places laid out than Bex had ever thought possible. It was like she had stepped in to a fairy tale. Or an incredibly expensive wedding venue. All around them, people milled around in the ballroom, glasses of whisky and champagne in hand.

'Kieron!' Lorna said excitedly at the sight of their host.

As his head turned in their direction, a smile flashed across his face.

'Glad you could all make it,' he said, looking at the group, before focusing her attention on Bex. 'You look beautiful, Rebecca,' he said as he kissed her gently on the cheek, before stepping back as if he needed to fully take her in.

'Thank you,' she replied.

Something prickled uncomfortably behind her skin. It was a perfect, gentlemanly gesture, and yet it was so different from the way it had been earlier with Duncan. Duncan had barely grazed her skin, and yet her whole body had rushed with heat, so much so that his very presence had consumed her. She'd wanted nothing more than to grab him, pull him close and never let him go. Whatever this was with Kieron, it wasn't the same. Guilt built within her. Kieron was a catch, and he would make someone a very lucky woman, but she didn't think that was going to be her.

'Don't forget about our dances later,' he said. 'But now, I'm afraid I have work to do.'

'Of course,' Bex said.

As Kieron turned back to the main hall, she noticed the waiter walking around with a tray of champagne and found herself desperate to down one. Yet before she could attract their attention, Kieron was knocking his ring against his glass, sending a chime out into the air.

'Ladies and gentlemen, if you would like to take your seats, please.' Kieron's voice rose above the chatter. 'It is time to welcome you to your places.'

With no idea what to expect, Bex had assumed they would all just take seats wherever they wanted, yet as she walked towards the dining table, she saw little name plaques in front of each seat. It was then that she realised she had neither accepted nor declined Kieron's offer to be her date for the night. For a brief second, she feared she would be seated next to him. Thankfully, she was a couple of places down, but nowhere near any of her friends. On her left was a slightly older man, and on her right, a woman a couple of years younger than herself.

'Yohan Dunsire,' the man said in a broad Scottish accent as he extended his hand. 'Local police commissioner.'

'Oh. Rebecca Barker,' Bex replied, feeling the need to give her full name. 'Accountant. Though, you can probably tell from the accent that I'm not a local.'

Yohan's overly bushy eyebrows twitched slightly. 'Ye the lass who did all the work for Fergus?'

'Yes,' Bex said. 'That's me.'

'Hmm. I thought you'd left. Heard you and the groundskeeper broke up, too.'

Bex felt a muscle twitch in her jaw. There was really no chance of privacy here. It was absolutely insane how much people knew. Even people she'd never met before. And if it was this bad for her, she could only imagine what it must have been like for Duncan. 'Yes, I did leave last summer,' she replied, hoping that the police commissioner would understand that her private life wasn't a conversation point for the evening. 'I'm just back to help with a few things. You know. With Fergus and everything...'

'Right, yes. Terribly sad. Good man, Fergus. A very good man indeed.'

As the chatter continued, Bex learned that the woman beside her was a journalist, someone Kieron knew from London, who must have said the word 'vibe' at least six times in her first sentence. Beyond the people she had come with, Bex recognised a few faces, including, unsurprisingly, Moira, Horace – Roddy's father – and several others from the pub. But from where she was seated, it was impossible to see over half of the guests, and she couldn't help but wonder if Gordon had decided to come or not. As for Duncan, there was no way Kieron wouldn't have invited him, given everything he did for the estate. That would just be churlish. Whether Duncan would show his face was another matter.

'Ladies and gentlemen.' Kieron clinked on his glass again as he rose at the head of the table. Hush fell over the dining hall as everyone turned to look at him. 'Thank you for joining me here at Highland Hall. I know today is a day shrouded by sadness, so I want to start by raising a toast to the man we all knew and loved. My beloved uncle, Fergus.'

The glasses went into the air.

'To Fergus!'

Date or no date, Bex appreciated Kieron's choice of toast.

Mentioning Fergus at the very start of the evening was, in her opinion, absolutely the right thing to do, and he wasn't finished.

'There are many here who knew him better than I did,' Kieron continued as the toasts subsided. 'And that is my shame. It is my shame that our lives took us so far apart until now. But I hope, with you all here beside me, you'll help me learn about this man whose role I will try to deserve, and whose gift of this lordship I will honour.'

Emotion swept across the table. Moira stared absentmindedly into her glass while the man beside her was dabbing his tears with a handkerchief.

'Tonight is to be a night to remember, but also to look forward,' Kieron said. 'Not just to my future, as laird, but to the future here at Highland Hall. A future I am sure you will all play no small part in.'

As the table raised their glasses for the second toast of the evening, the future, Bex couldn't help but wonder what Fergus would've said if he were here. Kieron was certainly more loquacious than the old laird had been. In fact, she struggled to imagine how Fergus would even begin a toast. Not to mention, in all the time she had known him, she could only ever recall seeing him in his wax jacket and flannel shirts. The thought of him in a suit was almost enough to make her chuckle. Still, she clinked her glass against those next to her, took another sip of her drink and waited for the remainder of Kieron's speech.

'Now there are many people I have to thank for bringing this night together under such short notice,' Kieron continued, 'and I will get to those names in a moment. But first, there is someone I would like to thank on a more personal level. Someone who went above and beyond. Rebecca Barker.'

As the eyes of the room turned to her, Bex felt her cheeks colour.

'I am sure that all of you who are local to the village will recall what an extraordinary job she did helping my uncle here. And, fingers crossed' – his eyes met hers, that twinkle brighter and bolder than she had ever seen before – 'she will continue to help me in my role here, too. To Rebecca.'

'To Rebecca!'

A chorus of cheers erupted, echoing her name. Bex wished she could shrink into her seat, and trying to keep her smile in place, she raised her glass. She wasn't sure she'd ever been toasted before. At work, maybe, and on her birthday, but never like this. But as much as she wished she could cower away, she knew that would help nothing. And so she met Kieron's gaze with the best smile she could muster.

As the cheers died down and Kieron continued with his list of thanks, the journalist next to her leaned in.

'God, what I wouldn't give to have him look at me like that,' she said quietly. 'You are one lucky woman to be tapping that.'

'We're not... we're not...' Bex stammered. 'There's nothing going on. I've just been helping him with some finance things.'

'Oh, sure.' The woman smirked. 'It's all platonic, of course. That's why he's encouraging everyone to join your accountancy firm. It's your skills, right?' She air-quoted the last word.

Bex's jaw tightened. 'It's probably because I'm a bloody good accountant,' she replied coolly, deciding she'd talk to the police chief for the rest of the meal, even if the bushiness of his eyebrows was somewhat distracting.

A few minutes later, the toasts were done, and Kieron was finally finishing up his speech.

'So I know we've got lots of hungry people here,' he said, the glass in his hand almost empty. 'And lots of talented people in great voice, who want to sing for us. So, with no further ado, I'd like to start us off with the "Selkirk Grace".'

40

Bex was more than surprised when, after the small but poignant 'Selkirk Grace', the pipe music resumed and people rose to their feet and began clapping.

'What's happening?' she hissed to Yohan.

'They're Piping in the Haggis,' he replied.

The haggis? Bex craned her head to see where the music was coming from, and it was only when the piper came into view that Bex realised he wasn't alone. He was indeed followed by a small woman, who was carrying a silver platter on which sat several large haggises.

A round of applause filled the room, gradually turning into louder rhythmic clapping, which only ceased when a loud cheer erupted as the haggises were ceremoniously placed on the table.

'Now, I shall read "Address to a Haggis",' Kieron announced.

'He's going to read a poem to a haggis?' The journalist beside Bex gawped.

'Yes,' Bex said curtly, ignoring the fact that she, too, had been more than a little surprised by this.

It was hard to take her eyes off Kieron as he spoke. He really was magnificent in the role of laird, and as he recited the Robert Burns poem, with his voice commanding and full of expression, a wide grin filled his face. The type of grin she'd rarely seen him share in the castle. Perhaps things had changed after she'd kissed him, not that she wanted to think too deeply about that. This smile reminded her far more of the man she had met at the airport.

When he finished, a hearty round of applause followed, and more toasts were raised. This time to the haggis itself.

Bex doubted she'd ever toast food again after this day, and yet the moment felt phenomenal. The mood was celebratory, almost wedding-like, and the food was delicious. So much so that some-where during the meal, she forgot that she hadn't wanted to talk to the journalist, and happily listened to her prattle on about the *vibe* of various other places she'd visited.

They started with cock-a-leekie soup, followed by haggis, neeps and tatties. For dessert, there was a tipsy laird, which Bex learned was a trifle drenched in alcohol. By the time the meal ended, Bex was feeling more than a little merry after all the wine she'd consumed, but whether it was because of the atmosphere, or because she'd only had one proper walk in days, she found herself desperate to keep going. To soak up every moment of the magnificent night.

She had just reached over to fill her glass when Kieron once again rose. There was no doubt he liked this part of the lairdship. The role of the host suited him. Maybe he didn't know much about the village or the land, but that could come with time. If he made enough of an effort.

'I hope you've enjoyed my food and hospitality,' he said, his cheeks slightly flushed with a hue of drink. 'But the evening isn't over yet. Please, dance, sing and have fun!'

Bex didn't need to be told twice and as she turned about in her chair, she saw Lorna already grabbing Eilidh and pulling her into the ballroom to dance. Ready to join them, she stood up, only to find her path blocked.

'Rebecca.' Kieron's eyes were practically sparkling as he looked at her. 'I hope you didn't mind my little toast earlier. I realised when I saw just how embarrassed you were that I probably should have checked you didn't mind me doing it first.'

'It was fine,' Bex said. 'Unexpected but fine.'

From the way Kieron's lips twisted, he clearly didn't believe her.

'Well, I promise not to do it again, without warning, but I do believe we agreed to a dance,' he said, offering his hand.

Her eyes moved across the room. If she was honest with herself, she knew exactly who she was looking for, but she was holding out no hope of seeing him. Still, it didn't matter. Duncan had made it clear how he felt about her, and tomorrow, when she was clear-headed, she would tell him the truth. She felt the same. She wanted to be with him. Whatever it took. Then they would sit down like adults and work out how they were going to make it work. After stripping each other naked, obviously.

But for now, the least she could do was dance with Kieron. After all, he was the person who had scooped her up out of the snow and carried her back here. And she liked him as a person. She would use the dance to friend-zone him in the nicest possible way, she decided. Explaining that the kiss had been, like he said, down to trauma and nothing more. He was a grown man. A gentleman even. He would understand.

As he took her hand, Bex felt the infectious energy of the room sparking through her. The room, and her new beginning. Perhaps she wouldn't even wait till tomorrow to talk to Duncan.

She would have a few dances and go find him. Yes, that was exactly what she'd do.

'One dance would be lovely,' she said and followed Kieron through to the ballroom.

41

As Bex moved over to the dancefloor, she couldn't help but notice that everyone else seemed to have picked up the moves immediately. A band was playing at the end of the room, a far cry from the ones she'd seen at Christmas dos or weddings. This group featured an accordion, a tin whistle and a fiddle. All the musicians were on their feet, dancing as they played. She'd seen something similar at a wedding once, but there had been an extra person there, someone who called out the moves they were supposed to follow. Here, there was none of that. Everyone just knew.

'I don't know what I'm meant to do,' she said, panic rising in her voice. The last thing she wanted to do was to sit out on the sidelines and miss out, but she didn't want to make a fool of herself either. 'I don't know these dances.'

'Don't worry.' Kieron smiled, seeming unperturbed by her confession.

'Look, it's not hard. Just follow me.'

He lifted his hand in the air and spun her outwards, but as he pulled her back in, his hand settled lightly on her waist.

'Will you look at that? You're a natural at this.'

Bex laughed. 'I'm not sure I'd go as far as to say that.'

'Trust me, you just do the same things over and over. You'll get it fast. I promise.'

Bex was caught between trying to watch what other people were doing and copying their moves without looking too far behind or treading on anyone's feet. It wasn't easy. Part way through the song, she thought she was getting the hang of things, and she jumped to the left, when the jump was meant to be to the right. The result was a collision with a tall, angular man who was dancing next to her.

'Just... maybe slightly smaller moves,' Kieron suggested.

A loud chuckle left her lips. It was hard to know whether the alcohol had helped or not. It definitely gave her confidence, although whether that was a good thing or not was debatable.

Regardless of how well Bex could do the actual dance moves, she couldn't remember the last time she'd had that much fun. Certainly not in a club. But it was far from conducive to the conversation she wanted to have with Kieron. Every time she got close enough to even consider talking, she was spun out again, or swung in for a sudden partner change, or simply too breathless to say anything at all.

Mid one spin she saw Gordon, standing at the edge of the dancefloor with a whisky in his hand, and another warmth spread through her, yet before she could acknowledge him, Lorna whipped past her.

'It looks like you two are having fun?' she said.

Bex tried to give her friend the look. The look that said yes, but this wasn't what she wanted. Or rather, who she wanted. Yet stopping dancing was easier said than done.

'You promised two, remember?' Kieron said as the first dance drew to a close.

'Of course.' Bex nodded, hoping that perhaps this one would be a little slower and that she could have the friend-zone conversation then. But if anything, the music was even quicker. Although thankfully the dance steps were easier to pick up, and she managed a full song without bumping into anyone.

As the second dance drew to a close, she was decided. She needed to talk to Kieron now. Nicely, kindly, but firmly. After all, the more dances she had with him, the more likely he was to think something was going to happen between them.

As the band finished and the applause rose into the air, she turned to look at him.

'You and I make quite a pair, don't you think?' he said, his hand still on her waist. There was something to the way his head was tilted to the side that made her think perhaps he was going to kiss her. And she couldn't let that happen. This was it. She knew it was. This was the moment she had to tell him she was spoken for. Yet as she opened her mouth to speak, another figure moved onto the dancefloor. He was here.

It was the first time she had ever seen him in full kilt and traditional attire, his long hair tied back in a bun at the base of his neck, and he took her breath away. He was gorgeous. A perfect specimen of a human, and he loved her. Her heart thudded in her chest as she tried to draw breath.

Applause for the musicians rippled around her, yet Bex stayed frozen, unable to move.

'Did you hear what I said?' Kieron asked. 'Are you ready for the next one?'

Bex knew she needed to reply. It was just basic manners. But she couldn't. It was like being in Lorna's cottage earlier that day. Her eyes were locked on Duncan's, and suddenly nothing else mattered.

'Actually,' Bex said, moving out of Kieron's grasp without a backwards glance, 'I have to go and talk to someone.'

42

Bex wasn't sure whether she walked all the way to Duncan, or whether he moved part way to meet her in the middle. It didn't matter either way. As she stood there next to him, she could only see him. It was as if the entire ballroom had evaporated from around them.

'Hey,' she said finally.

'Hey,' he replied.

Silence swirled around them again. The shrieks from the dancefloor melted into the ether.

'That's some moves you've got there—'

'About earlier—'

They spoke at the same time, and with a small laugh of relief, Bex encouraged him to go on.

'Sorry,' she said. 'You go first.'

She wasn't sure what she had been going to say, anyway. In fact, she was having difficulty holding any type of thought at all.

A familiar light pink tinge coloured his ears as a sheepish grin curled his lips. 'I was just going to say you've got some moves there. Not too sure about your choice of partner, but you looked good. Although I don't know how long my toes would stay intact, but you'll get better with practice. Maybe.'

'Hey!' she said, punching him playfully on the arm. Was it the first time she had touched him since she'd come back here? No, of course it wasn't. She'd helped carry him inside when he'd been drunk, and that had only been a week or so ago. But somehow, she had forgotten it. That night, those memories didn't matter any more. The future. That was what mattered.

'You looked beautiful. Look beautiful,' he corrected. 'You are so beautiful.' He said the words, so simply, so factually, as if only a fool could disagree.

Her stomach fluttered with a swarm of butterflies. She needed to say it, too. Not that he looked beautiful, but that she loved him. She had to tell him. But she didn't want to rush it. There was something about this moment that made her want to hold on to it forever.

'I wish I'd asked you to wear this before,' she said. 'I love the little purse thing, too.' She pointed to the small bag slung around his waist.

He rolled his eyes, but she could tell from the smirk on his lips that it was all in good fun.

'It's not a purse. It's a *sporran*,' he said. 'And I've told you that before.'

'Right,' she replied with a grin. Why couldn't she stop grinning? She was beyond ridiculous. 'So, do I get to know what you keep in it?'

Laughter lingered on his lips, but then it faded slightly and something far more sombre flickered across his expression.

'I keep a photo of my ma in it,' he said.

'Really?'

He nodded. 'I don't have many. But I remember my dad telling me once how she put a photo of herself in my first-ever sporran, and I've never taken it out. When she died... Well, it's just something I do now.'

'Can I see?'

All the time Bex had spent with Duncan, she'd only seen a couple of photos of his mother and most of those were family shots where she had her arms wrapped around him, half obscuring her face. Bex had got the feeling that she was the type of person who hadn't liked having her photo taken, just like Duncan, but now, she realised, she would make sure they took more of them together. For the family she hoped they would one day have.

Wordlessly, Duncan opened his sporran and pulled out a worn photograph.

'This was taken at a Burns Night,' he said, staring at it. 'I think that's actually one of the windows here in the background.'

He handed her the photo, which she took gently, and studied the image in front of her.

'So what do you think?' he said quietly.

Bex could feel Duncan's eyes boring into her, but at that moment, she had lost the ability to speak. Her eyes were fixed on the woman in the foreground. Not the simple black dress she was wearing, or the very nineties Rachel haircut. But her face. The roundness of her eyes. The curve of her loop.

As Bex stood there, she realised her pulse was racing, and a tightness wrapped around her chest.

'Bex,' Duncan said, placing his hand on her arm. 'Is everything okay? You look like you've seen a ghost.'

'I'm sorry, Duncan. Can I borrow this for a minute? I need to speak to Gordon.'

'Gordon?'

She nodded, struggling to swallow. 'Right. And Moira. I need you to find Moira and ask her to meet us in the study. I promise it'll make sense. Can you do that for me?'

'Can you tell me why?' Duncan asked. 'Why do you want that photo of my mother? What has she got to do with anything?'

But Bex didn't reply; she was already racing across the dance-floor in search of the lawyer.

43

Bex found the old lawyer standing by the bar, inspecting several bottles of whisky, presumably to work out which one he wanted to try next.

'Gordon, I need you. I need you now.'

'Bex.' He turned to look at her, while tapping one of the bottles, which the barman then picked up. 'Is everything all right?'

'I've found something. Something to do with the job. I think I know who it is. Who the heir is.'

The old lawyer frowned slightly, a small crease forming between his brows, but he didn't ask any questions. He followed her straight into the study.

'Crap!' Bex stopped abruptly, palming her forehead as she did.

'What is it?' Gordon asked. 'Are you sure you don't want to do this in the morning?'

'No, I want to do it now. We should do it. But the photo... the one with Fergus and the woman that I'd been meaning to show Moira, I left it at home.'

'You mean the one with Angus – Duncan's grandfather?'

'That's the one.' Bex considered the time. She could ring Roddy to run her back to the cottage quickly. It would be an annoying waste of time, but she couldn't be certain unless she had that photo.

'Oh, I took a snap of it,' Gordon said, opening up his own sporran. 'Just in case I saw her myself.'

'You did?'

'Aye, here it is.'

As Gordon flipped through his phone, Bex rushed forward and kissed him on the cheek. A full-on smack.

'Well, that was unexpected, but thank you. Now, what else have ya?'

With the photos sorted, Bex needed the last piece of the jigsaw puzzle. And she prayed like heck it would fit.

'There's a notebook,' Bex said as she began swinging open the cupboard doors. 'A small notebook with a list of hospitals in.'

The music continued out in the ballroom. The carefree sounds that, only moments ago, had felt so fun and made her feel so light were now boring into her mind, making it impossible to think.

'It wasn't random at all,' she said. 'I'm sure of it. They're not *random hospitals*. If I'm right... if I'm right... Got it!'

Her heart jolted in her chest as she opened up the notebook on the only written page.

'What?' Gordon asked. 'What is it, Bex? What have you found out?'

She shook her head, tears pricking behind her eyes. She couldn't tell him yet. Not until she was sure.

'We need to wait until Moira's here. She knows. The old woman knows. I'm sure of it.'

Moving over to the desk, she placed the notebook down and

opened it at the list of hospitals. Next to it, she placed the photograph Duncan had shown her only minutes before, the one of his mother, and Gordon's phone.

'You sure you don't want to let me in on all this?' Gordon asked, looking over at the desk. 'You know, given it's my job an' all?'

With her lips pressed tightly together, Bex considered that Gordon was right. She should probably tell him what she had discovered – or at least thought she had discovered – but before she could open her mouth, there was a knock at the door.

'Bex?' Duncan was standing there, his brow creased in worry. 'I found her for you.'

He stepped to the side, revealing Moira standing behind him, lips pursed. Bex hurried forwards and took the old woman by the hands.

'Moira, I need to ask you something, and I need you to tell me the truth. I think you already know what it is, don't you?'

The old lady shifted. Her gaze avoiding looking at the photo. And everyone else. 'My memory's not as good as it was, love.'

'Please don't do this. Please don't pretend you don't know what I'm talking about,' Bex said, her voice strained with urgency. 'It's too important for that.'

With a slight sniff, Moira nodded. A flicker of relief fluttered in Bex.

'Come on in. Sit down. We should shut the door.'

As Bex looped her arm into Moira's to help her into the room, Duncan cleared his throat.

'I guess I should leave you to it,' he said. 'The photo of my ma, though. If I could get it back from you?'

Bex shook her head. 'I'm sorry, Duncan. I don't think you should go anywhere just yet. You need to hear this, too.'

His mouth twitched, as if he was going to say something, but instead, he nodded once, then followed them into the room.

'Can you close the door?' Bex added as she lowered Moira into the armchair. 'We don't want to be interrupted.'

Wordlessly, Duncan closed the door, then moved silently into the room. Gordon had already taken a seat and Bex considered doing the same, only to find that she didn't want to sit down at all. She needed to move. She needed to keep moving.

'Okay, we're all yours,' Gordon said. 'What have you found out?'

Her heart was pounding and her throat was so dry she wished she'd brought a glass of champagne in with her. Not that she needed any more Dutch courage. She'd drunk enough for that already. But what she had seen, what she had figured out, wasn't because of the alcohol. She was sure of that. Clenching her fists at her sides, she drew a long breath. She was right. She knew she was.

After one more steeling breath, she opened her mouth, still not sure where exactly she was going to start.

'The thing is—' That was as far as she got as her words were cut short by the study door swinging open.

It felt as though the air had been sucked from the room as every pair of eyes turned to look at the man standing there in the doorway. A man who only a few minutes ago had been beaming at her. And yet now he was scanning the group with a look of mystified annoyance.

'Well, what exactly have we got going on here?' Kieron said.

44

Kieron moved further into the study, his expression relaxing slightly into a soft smile.

'There is a party going on, you know. And I was hoping to get another dance, Rebecca.'

The nerves Bex had been feeling multiplied a thousandfold, the adrenaline coursing through her veins so powerfully she could hear her pulse thrumming in her ears.

'I'm sorry, Kieron.' She tried to smile and look relaxed, but it was difficult. The desperate need to hear the truth from Moira's lips was making it nearly impossible to control the quiver in her voice. 'We just needed a quiet moment to discuss something. Something important.'

'So important that you're willing to miss out on free-flow champagne?' A slight laugh flittered from his throat, only to fade almost instantly when he noticed how no one reciprocated. As his smile wavered, his eyes darted between Bex and Gordon, then back again.

'This is about the will,' he said, any hint of good relation gone from his tone. 'If this is about the will, then I should be involved. This is my house. My inheritance. What is going on?'

Bex pressed her lips tightly together. Maybe doing this in the morning, when she was completely sober, would have been a better idea after all. Right now, the drink was making her desperate to blurt out the truth to Kieron. But that wouldn't be fair. Not to anyone. Not until they had their evidence.

'Please, Kieron.' She stepped towards him, her voice pleading. 'Gordon and I need to talk to Moira about something first. Please, let us do that. Let me see if I'm right before I jump to any conclusions.'

Kieron's gaze shifted to the old woman, who was still sitting in the armchair. Silent but surprisingly foreboding. Almost as if she was the matriarch of the castle. For a second, she thought Kieron might agree, but then he planted his hands on his hips.

'Then why is *he* here?' he said, pointing at Duncan.

'I dinnae know myself,' Duncan replied.

Bex clenched and unclenched her hands before letting out a slow exhale. 'It's complicated.'

'Well, if it's that complicated, and it's happening in *my castle*, then I should be involved. I'm not having secret meetings under my roof.'

It's not your roof, Bex wanted to scream, her nails digging into her palms as she fought to control herself. Emotions weren't going to help matters now, and she suspected they'd be running high soon enough. And not just hers.

'Okay,' she said finally, 'but I don't think you're going to like what you're about to hear.' Steeling herself, she added, 'I guess it's time for me to get started.'

Wishing she could stop her hands from trembling quite so much, she moved over to the desk and picked up Gordon's phone.

'Some of you will have seen this photo, some of you may not.'

She showed it first to Kieron, who stared at the screen with blank ignorance.

'What am I supposed to be looking at here?' he said.

'Well, I assume you recognise your uncle in this photograph? From his younger days.'

'Well, yes, yes, obviously.' His words were curt and Bex had no doubt that everyone in the room knew Kieron had not in fact recognised his uncle. She suspected he might not even know which of the two men he was. But still, she continued as if he had been truthful.

'Any idea who the people are with him?'

He shrugged, before handing the phone back to Bex. 'I assume they're people he used to hunt with. I don't know. He was always having photos taken with people. That's what happens when you're a laird. People want to have their photo taken with you.'

'Right.' Bex walked over to the armchair, where she gently laid the phone in Moira's hand. 'You know who they are, though, don't you, Moira? You know who all three of them are.'

The old woman's lips were already thinned with age, but when she pressed them together, they disappeared entirely. After a slight pause, she nodded.

'Aye,' she said. 'The other man's Angus Ramsay.'

'My grandfather,' Duncan said. Bex flashed him a quick smile, though Moira chose not to respond to the comment.

'What about the woman?' Bex continued. 'Who's she?'

Moira's gaze shifted down as she took a deep inhale, causing Bex's pulse to kick up yet another notch.

'That's Iona. Angus's sister.'

'Right, but that's not all she was. Is it?'

The tension in the room was growing with every heartbeat. Stretched so tight, Bex was sure that at any moment it might just snap and send everything unravelling. But she couldn't push Moira. She had held the secret for decades. She wasn't going to let it go easily.

'Sorry,' Duncan said, taking a step towards them. 'Did you say my grandad's sister? He didn't have a sister. He didn't have any siblings.'

He was looking at Moira as he spoke, but it was Bex who replied.

'The thing is, she didn't say she was your grandfather's sister, Duncan. She said she was *Angus's* sister.' She softened her voice. 'Moira, you can tell them. You can tell us all now. Nothing bad's going to happen.'

Moira's eyes pressed shut, her lips tight. 'We didn't like to gossip. We didn't,' she murmured. 'He was a good man—'

'But it's not gossip. This isn't gossip, Moira. This is justice. Surely you see that. If you don't tell the truth now... Moira, this is for Fergus. This is what he wanted. His will. His will says to his rightful heir. That's the word he used, Moira. *Rightful.* He wants his title to go to the person it belongs to.'

'What? What is all this nonsense about? I'm his heir. I'm his only nephew.' Kieron, who had remained so silent while Bex was talking to Moira that she'd almost forgotten he was there, strode towards her. 'Whatever this is, it stops now. So what if he worded it oddly? He was a doddery old man, with only dogs for company.'

A sound remarkably like a growl emanated from Gordon and Duncan simultaneously, though it was Gordon who spoke.

'Your uncle was the most rational man I ever met, all the way to his death. And he was certainly in sound mind when he wrote that. I should know. I was there.'

Kieron's jaw was locked, and there was no sign of a twinkle in his eye. Nothing but pure fury.

'This is ridiculous. You are not doing this. This is my house. My inheritance. I'm the rightful heir.'

Maybe it was the drink; maybe it was hearing Kieron sound so petulant. But whatever the reason, the restraint Bex had managed to maintain for the majority of the conversation snapped.

'No, you're not!' she shouted. 'Duncan is. Duncan is the rightful heir.'

'What?' Kieron's eyes locked on her, before a high-pitched laugh rattled from his lungs. 'What are you on about?'

'Look at this photo.' She grabbed the photo Duncan had handed her in the ballroom. 'What do you notice about it?'

Kieron huffed, sounding more like a toddler than a future laird. 'What is this? Another photo of Iona, I assume?'

'Sure as hell looks like it, doesn't it?' Bex couldn't help but let the smile twist at the corner of her lips. 'But it's not. It's Duncan's mother. There's a reason that she and Iona look so alike, though.' Bex swallowed, needing a breath before she could continue. 'The thing is, the man Duncan believes is his grandfather never had any children. Not one. But his sister did. Didn't she, Moira?' Bex looked solely at the old woman as she spoke. 'Iona had one child. Fergus's child. *Duncan's mother.*'

45

The music from the ballroom seemed to have faded. As if it was happening in a different time and space from where they stood. Or maybe that was just how it was for Bex. She could barely hear over the drumming of her own heartbeat.

All eyes were on Moira, waiting for her response. As they stood there, fearing she'd made a horrific mistake, Bex thought the silence might last forever, until Kieron let out a loud scoff.

'This is ridiculous,' he said. 'This is absolute nonsense. You're just trying to swindle me out of my inheritance!'

'Will you pipe down?' Gordon snapped. '*Your* inheritance? Like you've done anything to deserve it. Even if it weren't true, Duncan was more of a son to Fergus than you ever were.'

'But it *is* true, isn't it?' Bex urged, looking to Moira. She pulled the notebook from the desk.

'I thought this was strange when I went through it. All these hospital names, scribbled out and crossed through. But now I realise what he was doing. They're all maternity wards. Not random hospitals. Maternity hospitals. Fergus knew the truth. He was looking for her. Iona didn't get sick. She was pregnant, and she died in childbirth.'

'What?' Duncan's voice broke the stunned silence. It was the first time he'd spoken since Bex had revealed the truth. His look of disbelief was even greater than Kieron's.

'No... but my grandfather...'

Bex turned to face him, only now understanding the hurt that this would cause him. His grandfather had been his role model, his best friend, and now, their entire relationship had been built on a lie. This wasn't just about the inheritance. It was about so much more than that.

'The man you thought was your grandfather, Angus, was your *great-uncle*,' Bex said. 'You told me yourself how it was this big village scandal. How he disappeared and came back with this woman no one knew, and a baby. But she didn't stick around, did she? Apparently, she didn't bond with the baby – your mother. Not surprising really, given that she wasn't her child. It was never her child. It was never Angus's either. The baby was Iona's. Fergus and Iona's.'

'Nonsense!' Kieron spat. 'If that was the case, they would have said something. Laid claim to it straight away!'

'Not everything is about claiming money and castles, Kieron,' Bex said, her voice trembling. She wasn't sure why she felt tears trickling down her cheeks, but they were there. 'Angus was furious at what Fergus had done. He'd gotten his little sister pregnant, and she died because of it. He wasn't going to let him raise the child. But Angus needed the job. He needed the money. And he couldn't leave here. Fergus was heartbroken, and he needed to believe that Iona had got sick and died, because if it had been the pregnancy... if he had been the reason...' A deep throb burned through Bex's heart and she tried to contemplate all the pain the family had suffered. 'It was never about the money. It was about honour, family and love. I'm right, aren't I, Moira? I'm right about all of it.'

The old woman's lips were pressed tightly together, her chin dipped into her chest. Bex wasn't the only one crying, she saw. Tears streaked Moira's face.

Finally, she spoke, her voice wavering.

'There were aye gossips, of course. Folk reckoned he was taking advantage of her, wi' his position and all, but whenever I saw them... well, you know. You can tell, can't you? When two folk look at each other, you can tell when it's real.' She lifted her head and glanced at Bex, before shifting her gaze to Duncan and offering a slight smile, before she sniffed and continued. 'There were rumours, right enough. Apparently, he wanted tae marry her, but his folk wouldnae hear o' it. Him weddin' a groundskeeper's daughter and all that carry on. Still, he planned to do it anyway. She was an incredible woman. She really was.'

Moira's eyes softened as she looked at Duncan. 'Iona... your granny had a wicked sense of humour. Everyone loved her. She was a force of nature. Full of life. It's why we were all stunned when Angus told us she'd taken sick. Said she'd gone tae hospital, but were all vague wi' the details. I remember some sayin' it was Edinburgh, some others reckoned London. We didnae know. After she died, everyone was too sick with grief to worry about it. She was gone. That was all that mattered.

'And then Angus returned with this new woman and a wee bairn. Aye, there was gossip. An unmarried couple bringin' a baby in the house. None of us could work it out. And oh my, he would get fair cross if anyone mentioned Iona's name. Like he wanted to pretend she'd never existed.'

'I'm guessing the gossip from the new woman and the baby out of wedlock was enough to distract from Iona and Fergus,' Bex said.

Moira dipped her chin. 'Oh, there were those of us that suspected the truth. But we had too much respect for Fergus and Angus. And when that woman left, Angus did a grand job raising that wee girl on his own. He really did.' She looked at Duncan. 'He was a fine man. He was.'

'Fergus tried to tell you, Duncan,' Bex said, turning away from Moira and finally looking Duncan in the eyes. 'Fergus wanted you to know the truth. At the end he did. Lorna told me. You were away, right? Taking yourself off to get some space from him, and you couldn't get back in time. That's why he wanted *you* when he knew it was his final hours. That's why he tried to call you twelve times. Not anyone else in the family. You. Because he was going to tell you the truth. That you were his grandson.'

'Stop this!' Kieron's voice rose above them all. 'Stop this nonsense! It's an absolute farce. I see what you're doing. You want to be lady of the castle, and you think you can use your *boyfriend* to—'

'That is not what's happening here!' Bex snapped. 'This has nothing to do with any relationship we had in the past. This is what Fergus wanted. This is the truth. And this is what matters.'

A sly smirk twisted on Kieron's lips as he scoffed. 'Oh, I knew you were smart, Rebecca, but I never figured you were that conniving. Making a power-play to make sure you claim yourself as lady of the manor. First, you play with me. Kiss me and lead me on and then—'

'You kissed him?' Duncan looked like she had just slapped him across the face. 'You kissed him?'

It felt as though all the heat had drained from the room. She had started the evening knowing exactly what she wanted to do: tell Duncan she loved him and plan out a future together. How had it all gone so wrong?

'Please, this isn't about any of that right now. This is about the will.' She turned to Gordon. 'I'm sure I'm right,' she said. 'Will it be possible to find out?'

He nodded. 'A DNA test should be fairly straightforward. Yes. I'll speak to the firm and get it sorted tomorrow morning.'

'Well, just be aware that you'll be hearing from my lawyers,' Kieron said, his voice thick with fury. 'This whole business. This collaboration, this manipulation, this... fraud! You won't get away with it. Mark my words. And you...' He glowered at Bex. 'To think what I would have done for you.'

With that, he turned on his heel and stormed out of the room.

46

Silence followed in Kieron's wake. Bex wiped the tears that were now freely trickling down her cheeks. And she wasn't the only one. Even Gordon had removed his glasses to dab under his eyes.

'I'm sorry.' Bex choked out the words. 'I didn't mean for it to go like that. I just... I just...'

'It's fine,' Gordon said softly. 'You did the right thing here,' he added, looking at Moira. 'You both did the right thing.' He paused, and before the silence settled fully, he turned to Duncan. 'This is going to be a lot for you to take in. We'll give you two some space.' Slowly, he helped Moira to standing, but rather than heading for the door, she moved across to Duncan and rested her hand on his arm.

'It disnae change things, you know. The way your grandad – Angus – the way he loved you and your ma, it disnae change that.'

Duncan turned slightly and took the old woman's hand in his own. No words, just touch. That was all he could manage.

'We should leave them to it,' Gordon said, touching Moira

gently. A moment later, the pair left the room, closing the door gently behind them and leaving Bex and Duncan alone.

'Did you know?' she said, eventually. 'Did you ever have any idea?'

He shook his head, but somewhere during the motion, it turned into a shrug.

'He was a lonely old man, and I was a pretty lonely young man. I just thought that was all there was to it, really. You know, you might be wrong. My God, you're gambling your chances with Kieron if you're wrong about this.'

'I never wanted any chances with Kieron.' Bex took a step towards Duncan, only for his face to harden.

'Right. You just kissed him for fun?'

'I kissed him after I'd nearly frozen to death and you told me that it was a good thing that we split up,' she replied. 'You have no idea how what you said hurt me that day. And in case I'm mistaken, you've done a lot more than kiss someone since we split up?' The hurt sounded remarkably like anger in her voice. With a deep breath in, she tried her best to swallow it back down. This wasn't the time to talk about them. Duncan had bigger things to deal with.

Once again, silence took hold. How was it that only half an hour ago, Bex had been there on the dancefloor, ready to tell Duncan that she loved him, that she would do whatever she needed to make this relationship work and now she couldn't even find the strength to speak?

'I'm sorry.' Duncan inched towards her, his eyes locked on hers. 'I meant all of it. I meant everything I said earlier today. You know I did.'

'I know.'

'And you might not have said it yet, but I'm pretty sure you still love me, too.'

He lifted her hands and interlocked their fingers. She did. She loved him with every fibre of her body. So much so that her heart ached. A full, all-consuming pain, for which she knew the cure was standing only feet away from him. It would be so much easier to forget everything and lose herself in this moment. But she stopped him with her hand.

'Don't,' she said. 'Please don't.'

His frown crinkled. 'You don't want this?'

A lump had lodged itself firmly in Bex's throat, and swallowing did nothing to alleviate it. Still, she had to speak. 'You have too much going on right now. Too much to think about. This, what you learned tonight. It's gonna cloud your judgement. You don't want to do anything you'll regret.'

He let out a light laugh and brushed his thumb against her jawline. 'The only thing I regret is not putting a ring on your finger and keeping you in my life forever.'

A stifled gasp choked in Bex's throat. Was he saying what she thought he was saying? Yes, there was no ambiguity in those words. Duncan wanted to marry her. To be with her forever. And wasn't that what she wanted too? She knew it was. Yet, as she opened her mouth to respond, Kieron's words swirled in her head. How she was just making a power-play to be the lady of the manor. He had just raised a toast – his third toast of the entire meal – to her. He had made it seem like they were a thing. And the way they had danced together, straight after the meal? She could hardly blame anyone if they'd jumped to that conclusion.

If she told Duncan she loved him now, that she wanted to be with him, then what would everyone in the village think? That she had separated from him, only to suddenly find him more appealing now that he was worth millions? That she had toyed with Kieron when she'd assumed he would inherit Highland Hall, then flipped back to Duncan when it turned out he was the rightful heir? He would be a laughingstock. She couldn't do that to him.

'You've got bigger things to deal with,' she said, stepping back and out of his grip and trying to ignore the chill that spread across her skin. 'Your life's going to change. And we don't know if there's even a place for me in it any more.'

'What are you on about? There will always be a place for you. Always. Did you not listen to anything I said earlier?'

His gaze was locked on hers. His lips were only inches away.

'I don't think that's enough,' she said quietly. 'It's not right. I'm sorry. Honestly, I'm so, so sorry.'

Then, praying he couldn't see the tears prick behind her eyes, she turned and walked away from the only man she'd ever truly loved.

47

The next morning, Lorna was in bed nursing what was bound to be a catastrophic hangover while Bex sat on the sofa, her computer on her lap as she debated her life choices.

After her conversation with Duncan, Bex had headed straight home. The way she and Duncan had left things meant her party spirit had very much gone, and the thought of facing Kieron was enough to have her bolting for the door.

It had been another four hours before Lorna staggered in, full of song, not to mention questions about where she had disappeared to for so long and gossip about how drunk and moody Kieron had been when he'd finally kicked them all out. Even though Bex had still been wide awake when she'd heard the front door go, she'd hurriedly closed her eyes and proceeded to keep them closed as she responded to all of Lorna's comments with a series of low grunts, hopefully giving the impression she was either too drunk or too tired to answer them. Thankfully, Lorna had given up eventually, leaving Bex to toss and turn before finally falling asleep for real, hoping everything would be clearer in the morning.

It wasn't. And now she had been up for over two hours, staring at an email she'd written when she'd first woken, still unsure whether to send it.

It was the right thing to do, in her heart she knew that, but she just needed some reassurance. It was where to go for said reassurance that was the issue. Ruby had been sitting with her the entire time – other than when Bex had let her out the back door for a wee – but as brilliant a companion as Ruby was, in terms of advice, she was totally useless, meaning Bex needed to look elsewhere for help.

Bex knew there was no point in asking Lorna, or any of her friends in the village, not only because she already knew what their responses would be, but because it would raise a whole heap of questions that weren't hers to answer. They might only have subjective evidence for now, but she knew what the DNA test was going to show. She would bet everything she owned on it. And with the way village gossip spread, and the strop Kieron had thrown, she was pretty sure that by the end of the week, every resident of LochDarroch would know there was another potential heir in the mix. They might even know that Duncan was top of the suspect list. Which was why she couldn't say anything. Gossip was bad enough, but when it was someone you loved at the centre of it, someone whose entire life was about to be turned upside down, she refused to be a part of it. But for that same reason – Duncan's life being tossed into turmoil – she couldn't go back to London yet. Not until she knew he'd be okay.

With the phone in her hand, Bex debated ringing her parents. They gave sound advice, but would also have questions. What she needed was someone who would listen without prying. What she needed was her oldest friends. And thankfully, Daisy picked up straight away.

'Hey, is everything all right?'

'I'm not sure exactly,' Bex started, only for the tears to well behind her eyes. 'Actually, no. It's all a complete mess.'

'Bex, what is it? What's happened? What do you need?'

What did she need? She had no idea. To go back in time and make sure Duncan was there to take Fergus's phone call, so that she'd never been dragged into all this. Or further back in time still, so that they'd never broken up and she could have been there, at his side, to help him deal with it all.

She sniffed, trying to swallow back the tears as she choked out her reply.

'I think... I think I just need to take some time off work. A couple of weeks. Things here with the will... it's complicated. I'm not sure I can come back yet.'

'Then don't.' Daisy was straight to the point. And just like Bex had hoped, there were no prying questions asking exactly what was complicated or why it had her in such a state. 'Why don't you speak to Nigel? You've sacrificed more than enough for that company. He owes you. I'm sure he'll give you as long as you need.'

Bex swiped at her continuous stream of tears with the back of her hand, only to find it lacked any form of absorbency, and so picked up a pillow and used that instead.

'You're right, you're right,' she said. 'I'm sorry for ringing. I'm just being silly.'

'No, you're not. If you need anything, let me know.' Daisy paused, and Bex could hear the question teetering at the end of her tongue. But she didn't ask it. 'Whatever this complication is, you'll be okay. I promise,' she said instead.

'I hope so. Love you.'

'Love you too.'

The second Bex hung up the phone, she didn't give herself a chance to think. Instead, she tossed the pillow to the side, grabbed her laptop and clicked send on the email. There it was. Sent. Now, all she could do was wait and see, and that wasn't something she wanted to do inside.

'Come on, girl,' she said, scratching the super-soft patch of fur behind Ruby's ears. 'Let's go for a walk.'

On the off-chance that Lorna did wake up before she was back, Bex wrote a note, saying what time she'd left, what time she expected to be back and assuring her that she would be sticking to the main roads around the village, so there would be people close by should anything happen. While it felt a little unnecessary to write such a thing, she knew she'd already put her friends through so much; this felt like the least she could do.

Outside, it was a crisp, clear day, where the white fluffy clouds and bright blue sky could have easily been mistaken for a summer's day had it not been for the biting cold and glinting frost on the grass. The two walked silently and slowly until they reached the turn down to the castle. Only then did Bex stop as she gazed down the path.

Last night, leaving Duncan alone and giving him space to digest what he'd just learned had felt the kindest thing to do. But now she was second-guessing that decision. The last thing she wanted was for him to feel like she wasn't there for him when he needed her. But then what good would that do when she couldn't be there for him long term? Unless Nigel came back and agreed to her request, she might have to be on a flight back to London before the weekend.

A deep throb burned through her chest as Ruby let out a slight whine and tugged the lead.

'It's best if we stay away for now, girl,' Bex said as she cast one more glance down the lane, let out a sigh, then carried on back up to the village.

Given that she'd not yet had a message or call from Lorna,

Bex assumed she was still asleep. She was also pretty sure that Lorna had a shift at the pub later, and if she wasn't up soon, there was no chance she was going to make it.

Deciding that perhaps food was the best way to rouse her current housemate, and knowing that there was very little in the cottage, she headed to the café.

Judging by the number of heads hanging in the village, Lorna wasn't the only one nursing a hangover and when Bex pushed open the café door, the aroma of coffee was even stronger than usual, though there was surprisingly little chatter, and even the tinkle of the bell of the door was enough to make some of the patrons flinch. However, behind the counter was a familiar, yet unexpected, face.

'Roddy? What are you doing here?'

Roddy had been the one to drive Bex home from the castle well before the festivities drew to a close. In his normal diplomatic way, he hadn't said anything as silent tears streamed down her cheeks, other than to check she was okay. But she knew that he'd waited outside the cottage until she was inside, before heading back to continue ferrying people home.

'What do you think?' he said, flashing her a smile. 'I'm the only one clear-headed enough to work. And today of all days, people need their caffeine.'

He nodded over to a table, where one patron was slumped over, a coffee cup in each hand and a teapot in the middle.

'Yeah, Lorna's pretty worse for wear,' Bex said. 'Was hoping I could grab a couple of bacon rolls to take back?'

'Sure thing. Just take a minute. Want to take a seat while you wait?'

'Thanks.'

After picking up a water bowl for Ruby, Bex moved over to a table by the window. Her eyes drifted outside. She should message Duncan, she thought. Just send him a quick text to say she was here if he wanted to talk. After all, he hadn't even had the time she'd had to consider the possibility of there being another heir to Fergus's estate, let alone that it could be him. That kind of shock would shake anyone. Even someone as level-headed as Duncan. Messaging was what a friend would do. If they couldn't be more than that, then friends was what she'd have to settle for.

Deciding there was no time like the present, she picked up her phone, only for it to start buzzing in her hand. Her heart knocked against her ribs at the sight of her boss's name.

'Hi, Nigel.' There was a definite quiver in her voice. A nervousness. If he didn't approve her request, then she wasn't exactly sure what she'd do.

'Rebecca, I got your email.'

Her pulse quickened further still. 'Yes, I know it's a lot to ask—'

'No, no. I understand. It's been a tough time for you. So a month sabbatical, that's what you're saying you'd like?'

'Yes, yes, please.' She swallowed a lump in her throat, unsure where it had come from. She was normally so confident in work conversations. It was difficult to know why this one was different. 'I know it's not typical.'

'Let's be honest, there have been lots of things about your last few years that have been less than typical. It's fine. Honestly, with all the business you've brought this way the last week, I don't think anyone will have any issues, and I'll have to talk through all the details with HR but it shouldn't be any problem. Take your month. That corner office will be waiting for you when you get back.'

'Really?' The relief that flooded from her chest was almost enough to make her want to cry. 'Thank you, Nigel. Thank you so much.'

'Just make sure you don't stay up there permanently. This place'd be lost without you.'

'Don't worry,' Bex replied, unable to stop herself from grinning. 'I'll be back.'

Only once she'd hung up the phone did Bex sit back in her chair and digest what this meant. One month. A little over four weeks, to get everything in order and make sure that this time, when she headed back to London for good, she was finally ready to move on with her life without Duncan in it. It sounded so simple when she thought of it that way. Who knew, maybe it would be...

* * *

MORE FROM HANNAH LYNN

The next book in the Highland Hall series from Hannah Lynn, *Love and Lairds at Highland Hall*, is available to order now here:

https://mybook.to/LoveandLairdsBackAd

ABOUT THE AUTHOR

Hannah Lynn is the author of over twenty books spanning several genres. Hannah grew up in the Cotswolds, UK. After graduating from university, she spent 15 years as a teacher of physics, teaching in the UK, Thailand, Malaysia, Austria and Jordan.

Download your exclusive bonus content from Hannah Lynn here:

Visit Hannah's website: www.hannahlynnauthor.com

Follow Hannah on social media:

       f facebook.com/hannahlynnauthor
       ⧉ instagram.com/hannahlynnwrites
       BB bookbub.com/authors/hannah-lynn